THE MARK OF KANE

Though this play is inspired by actual historical events, it is a work of fiction. All of the characters, events, and organizations portrayed in this work are either products of the author's imagination or used fictitiously. In certain case incidents, characters and timelines have been changed for dramatic purposes. Certain characters may be composites, or entirely fictitious.

The Mark Of Kane

Copyright © 2022 by Mark Pracht

ISBN-13: 978-1957328508

Cover art by Tony Donley

For information about production rights, contact:
mark.pracht@gmail.com

Published by Sordelet Ink

THE MARK OF KANE

A PLAY BY
MARK PRACHT

PART ONE OF THE FOUR-COLOR TRILOGY

Dedication

For Colene, who always reminds
me that I can.

And Bill.

THE MARK OF KANE was originally produced at City Lit Theatre in Chicago, IL from Oct 21st, 2022 to December 4th, 2022. Directed by Terry McCabe, Stage management by Zachary Osterman, Scenic, Lighting and Projection Design by G. "Max" Maxim IV, Costume Design by Rachel S. Parent, Original Music composed by Petter Wahlback, and Original Artwork created by Tony Donley.

The original cast was as follows:

Bob Kane — Josh Zagoren

Bill Finger — Todd Wojcik

Portia Epstein-Finger — Annie Hogan

Arnold Drake — Adam Bitterman

Jerry Robinson — Lee Kanne

Sheldon "Shelly" Moldoff — David Valenta

Jim Steranko — Michael Sherwin

Vin Sullivan / Charles Sinclair — Sean Harklerode

Tessie Finger/Agusta Kahn/Lilly Uslan — Laura Coleman

Louis Finger/Herman Kahn/Jack Liebowitz/William Dozier — John Wehrman

Lottie/Gilda Finger/Doris Kahn/Michael Uslan/ Veronica — Zoe Deprez

Harry Donenfeld/Sam Singer — Linsey Falls

Randy/Fred Finger/Jerry Bails — Dakota J. Pariset

Cast of Characters

Bob Kane
Bill Finger
Arnold Drake
Jerry Robinson
Shelly Moldoff
Jim Steranko
Jerry Bails
Portia Epstein/Finger
Vin Sullivan
Randy
Gilda Finger
Tessie Finger
Louis Finger
Agusta Kahn
Herman Kahn
Doris Kahn
Harry Donenfeld
Jack Liebowitz
Sam Singer
Fred Finger
Lottie
Michael Uslan
Lilly Uslan
Veronica
Charles Sinclair
William Dozier

"Comics are one of the five native American art forms, including banjo music, jazz music, musical theatre, and the mystery story as invented by Edgar Allen Poe."

— Harlan Ellison

"Comics are the bastard offspring of art and commerce."

— Art Spiegelman

FOREWORD

The first thing I ever read entirely on my own, if I can trust my memory (unlikely), was the January 1979 issue of the seminal DC Comics Batman team-up title, THE BRAVE AND THE BOLD, co-starring the "faceless hero of World War II," The Unknown Soldier. That's issue 146, if you want to go look it up.

I. Was. Hooked.

When I first made the pilgrimage to San Diego, California, for the annual gathering of the tribes known popularly as the San Diego Comic-Con International, it was 2006. I had read all the books, and I knew all the names, Siegel, Schuster, Lee, Kirby, and, of course, Bob Kane. So when I walked into the small convention meeting room for the "Golden Age Batman Panel," I was prepared for fun anecdotes and tales about the great man who dreamed up The Dark Knight. The dapper gentleman posing in the pictures from the set of all the Batman movies, and in the Warner Brothers Store catalog, wearing that badass silk Batman jacket (I was a DEEPLY dorky young man) and bat-logo ball cap.

I didn't get that.

What I got was comic book royalty, artists Jerry Robinson and Sheldon Moldoff, and writers like Arnold Drake, speaking openly about the failings of Bob Kane. Stories of credit for work done by others, personal mythologizing, and selfishness that somewhat broke my heart. They also mentioned another name:

Bill Finger.

Flash forward to 2012, where I attend yet another San Diego Comic-Con panel, this one featuring Marc Tyler

Nobleman, speaking about his illustrated book (with artist Ty Templeton) for young people called BILL THE BOY WONDER: THE SECRET CO-CREATOR OF BATMAN. I listened in rapt attention, to the tales of a full-hearted creative voice that, while not completely forgotten, was left behind as Kane's myth grew and grew. On my flight back from San Diego with my traveling companion, I turned to him and said, "There's a play in this."

My lifetime of love for these four-color wonders mixed with my decades of toil in storefront theatre (with a few stops in actual, honest-to-god "living wage" work), and came to a head when a global pandemic put me in a position of sitting at home, craving something creative. The result was the play you've purchased (thank you!), as well as the following two scripts that will encompass "The Four-Color Trilogy." More on that later.

This play is a fiction, details and timelines have been adjusted for dramatic effect, and it really only tells half the story. I encourage you, if you are compelled by Bill and Bob's story, to seek out the books, websites and documentaries that have been released to tell the full story.

Notes

This story is loosely based on actual events and people. In certain case incidents, characters and timelines have been changed for dramatic purposes. Certain characters may be composites, or entirely fictitious.

SUPERMAN, BATMAN and associated characters are copyright and trademark of DC Comics. They are used in historical context, and no ownership is implied.

COURAGEOUS CAT and MINUTE MOUSE are copyright and trademark Telefeatures, LLC. They are used in historical context, and no ownership is implied.

THE SHADOW is copyright and trademark Conde' Nast Publishing. The character is used in historical context, and no ownership is implied.

"Alone" by Edgar Allan Poe, as well as selections from "A Princess of Mars" by Edgar Rice Burroughs, "The Hound of the Baskervilles" by Arthur Conan Doyle, "The Devil in Iron" by Robert E. Howard, and "Tarzan of the Apes" by Edgar Rice Burroughs are public domain and no ownership is implied.

A note on projections: These should be dynamic, brief, and not intrude into the scenes. Dialogue should be continuous.

The Mark of Kane

ACT I

SCENE ONE

(Lights rise, revealing a line of older men, JERRY ROBINSON, SHELLY MOLDOFF, ARNOLD DRAKE, and the moderator, an extremely dashing JIM STERANKO, standing. Projected: The San Diego Comi-Con "Eye" Logo)

STERANKO
So welcome all to San Diego, California, and this year's Comic-Con International! Now I know most of you kids out there are frothing at the mouth to hear from our guests, but the powers-that-be have, in their infinite wisdom, picked me to host this little confab, so you gotta listen to my gab, too!

(Projected: 2006)

DRAKE
Hear that Jerry? Don't speak unless spoken to.

ROBINSON
Dear God, didn't anybody warn them about putting Steranko on a stage?

MOLDOFF

You're looking good, Jim.

DRAKE

Oh, he knows it, Shelly.

STERANKO

All right, all right, enough of the ball-busting, boys. I finally have you all right where I want you...

DRAKE

You gonna slap us around?

ROBINSON

Congrats on that, by the way. Needed to be done.

STERANKO

Ancient history, my friend, nothing that these kids want to hear about.

DRAKE

Well, it is a Batman panel, your...shall we say... striking...

(The guys chuckle)

DRAKE

...Run-in with MISTER Robert Kane might be of interest.

MOLDOFF

(Whispers to ROBINSON) What's he talking about?

STERANKO

A tale for another time. Right now, I want to get into the deep end with you fellas! Batman royalty! Jerry Robinson, legendary Batman artist...

ROBINSON

...Creator of The Joker!

STERANKO
Sheldon Moldoff, prolific artist of the early Batman adventures.

MOLDOFF
Ahh, just Shelly.

STERANKO
And Arnold Drake, creator of the Doom Patrol, and contributing Batman writer.

DRAKE
Present!

STERANKO
And I am your humble host, Jim Steranko!

DRAKE
"Humble!"

(The guys chuckle warmly)

STERANKO
Three titans of the Golden Age, seminal figures in the history of the Dark Knight, all here to drop the straight dope! Isn't that just the cat's pajamas!

(STERANKO juices the audience)

STERANKO
Let's get to the brass tacks, boyos!

DRAKE
We were there. In the trenches, so to speak.

ROBINSON
We did the work.

STERANKO
A brotherhood of creative enterprise. Spilling ink and blood onto the page.

MOLDOFF

It was a job. Silly little stories for kids. Who knew anybody'd care five months later, let alone six decades?

ROBINSON

Speak for yourself, Shelly.

DRAKE

Jerry here had a sense of his own importance from way back.

STERANKO

I know the feeling.

ROBINSON

(To DRAKE) Here it comes.

MOLDOFF

All I wanted was to feed my family.

STERANKO

I hear that. When I was criss-crossing the country, breaking locks and chains, a hot meal was everything. My whole life, even when things were relatively stable at Marvel doing Nick Fury...But! That! Is a tale for another time.

ROBINSON

But why NOT talk about your accomplishments?

DRAKE

Yes, oh great Steranko, tell us about yourself!!

ROBINSON

(To DRAKE) You owe me ten bucks.

STERANKO

These boys know me too well.

(Laughs)

STERANKO
The hash on the table today is the Batman, so, we better start with the name on all those books. I'm speaking about a man who's become a face enshrined on the Mount Rushmore of comics...Bob Kane.

(There is a moment as the men think about what to say)

MOLDOFF
Bob was...

DRAKE
He knew how to look out for himself.

STERANKO
History has named him the father of a character that is, arguably, the most famous superhero in history.

MOLDOFF
Bob saw what people wanted, what would sell.

DRAKE
You remember the clown paintings?

MOLDOFF
Oh dear lord...

STERANKO
This sounds like a story.

DRAKE
In the '60s there was this fad of these God-awful sad clown paintings...

ROBINSON
That Red Skelton garbage?

DRAKE
God knows there is no accounting for the junk the public will buy into...So Bob started selling these clown paintings. All signed, very large, "Bob Kane."

ROBINSON
Swore he was going to make out like a bandit.

DRAKE
It was more than money to Bob. He was so proud of the damn things, "Forget Batman! This is going to make me in the world of art."

STERANKO
Oh, baby, you've got to be kidding.

DRAKE
"These paintings will soon be in every gallery in the world." He thought the Louvre was going to take down the Mona Lisa and put up his clown paintings.

MOLDOFF
Bob had a knack, he knew a promising bandwagon when he saw one.

STERANKO
But we know he had a lot of ghosts. All three of you guys were doing work under his name.

MOLDOFF
Ehh, a lot of guys had studios. Whole teams working under their credit. Eisner and Iger, Simon and Kirby, Siegel and Schuster. Everybody did it.

ROBINSON
That wasn't exactly the same thing, Shel...

STERANKO
That leads us to another name...Bill Finger. Someone we all knew, but, sadly, a lot of these ankle-biters out here may not...

ROBINSON
And they should.

DRAKE
No doubt of that.

ROBINSON
(To audience) Every. One. Of you out there, if you love comic books, you should know Bill Finger.

STERANKO
Absolutely! Do we know how Kane and Finger met?

ROBINSON
It was a party Bob was throwing, wasn't it?

DRAKE
Well…That's what Bob said…

(Lights shift)

Scene Two

(A party is underway. A female guest, LOTTIE, held in the sway of the host, elegantly decked out in an ascot and smoking jacket, this is BOB KANE)

(Projected: 1939)

KANE
Do you need a top-off, Lottie?

LOTTIE
This apartment is so nice, Bob. I live in a third-floor walk-up closet over in Queens! I'd kill for this place!

KANE
I'm moving to a larger place uptown in a few weeks. If you play your cards right, Lottie, you just might get to spend a night or two here before I vacate.

LOTTIE
Oh BOB! You scoundrel!

KANE
Ah-ha! "Is the prison that Mr. Scoundrel lives in at the

end of his career a more uncomfortable place than the workhouse that Mr. Honestly lives in at the end of his career?"

KANE
Bob, I don't know what to do with you!

(LOTTIE exits. Another man enters, BILL FINGER, his dress is clean, but simple, a notebook is jammed into his jacket pocket)

FINGER
Wilkie Collins?

KANE
Who?

FINGER
Wilkie Collins. You just quoted THE WOMAN IN WHITE..."Women can resist a man's love, a man's fame, a man's personal appearance, and a man's money..."

KANE
In my experience, money is not on that list.

FINGER
"...but they cannot resist a man's tongue when he knows how to talk to them."

KANE
I don't follow.

FINGER
Wilkie Collins wrote that.

KANE
Does it matter? All I can say is, any line that justifies a little perversion is worth stealing.

FINGER
Oh, is it?

KANE
Women like to play at virtue, but it isn't nearly as much fun as when a rich man wants to take you to bed. Especially if you wrap it in poetical nonsense. Just *act* like you're rich. It's not like she's an accountant.

FINGER
But...

KANE
Lottie? What she doesn't know...

FINGER
I have to admit, I haven't tried straight-up lying.

KANE
Lying? No, no, my friend. Anticipation. Someday, I AM going to have that stately manor outside of town, butler, fancy cars...

(*LOTTIE passes by and giggles*)

KANE
...And any woman I want.

FINGER
How do you plan to do that, mister...?

KANE
Kane, Bob Kane.

FINGER
Bill Finger.

KANE
In the next few years? The name Kane will be right up there with Chester Gould and Walt Kelly.

FINGER
Comic strips?

KANE
Cartooning, please.

FINGER
Really? I'm trying to break in, too. I've got stacks of Shadow and Doc Savage back at my apartment.

KANE
Pulps? Those are on their last legs, Bill.

FINGER
Can't argue. Siegel and Schuster? Those guys changed everything. Can you believe the way Superman has taken off?

KANE
Schuster's a hack. I'm more of a Milton Caniff acolyte.

FINGER
Well, yeah! I mean, the newspaper strips are the gold standard. Everybody knows those guys!

KANE
Exactly, Caniff's the master.

FINGER
Look at Hal Foster, that's just gorgeous work, but there's no dynamics. Too static. Al Capp? It's gorgeous, but never feels real. Caniff...he's the king.

(KANE regards him for a moment)

KANE
Your name is Bill?

FINGER
Right.

KANE
You changed it?

FINGER
(Laughs) Well, c'mon, Bob, who hasn't?

KANE
Milton.

(Beat)

FINGER
I hate that name.

KANE
DeWitt Clinton High School. You were a senior in my second year.

(KANE pours FINGER another drink)

KANE
A toast to the alma mater!...I'm over at the Eisner and Iger studio, now.

FINGER
Eisner and Iger? Really? They're...

KANE
It's a temporary situation, I assure you. Taking all the work I can get, working my way up. I have some contacts over at National, they've been sniffing around a strip I have, "Rusty and His Pals."

FINGER
I'm a writer, myself. I've got...a few things...here and there...I've been working on, too.

KANE
Doesn't everyone. Where have you been published?

(FINGER pulls his notebook from his pocket)

FINGER
I have a lot of ideas! A ton of gimmicks, really. Anything

I see or hear that I think I can use, I write it down here. Jokes, images, anything that can spark a story.

KANE
But have you been published?

FINGER
Not...yet.

KANE
Where have you submitted?

(Beat)

FINGER
I'd just love to write for the pulps, have my own Shadow like Walter Gibson, or John Carter like Burroughs.

KANE
Can I give you some advice, Bill?

FINGER
I'd love it.

KANE
"Whatever you can do or dream you can, begin it. Boldness has genius, power and magic in it. Begin it now."

FINGER
Sounds like Goethe.

KANE
Whatever, it's sound advice.

FINGER
You really think quoting a German is the smartest thing right now?

KANE
What do you mean?

FINGER
Goethe. He's German...

(Beat)

FINGER
The trouble in Europe?

LOTTIE *(off-stage)*
Bahhhb! Come dance with me!

KANE
This may be a high-class party, Bill, but I don't think these folks know...what was it? Goethe?

LOTTIE *(off-stage)*
Bahhhb!!

KANE
Let alone where he was from.

(LOTTIE enters, and tugs on KANE)

LOTTIE
Bahhhbeee!!

FINGER
You may have a point.

KANE
My dear, I am conversing with a fellow artist. I promise I'll cut a rug with you right after.

LOTTIE
You better!

KANE
Have I EVER lied to you, my dear?

(LOTTIE exits)

LOTTIE *(off-stage)*
Who has more champagne?!

(FINGER takes in the room)

FINGER
Nice girl, nice apartment. Comics must pay better than
they say.

KANE
This isn't your apartment?

(Beat)

FINGER
Have you said anything truthful tonight?

KANE
Bill, the truth is I can use a guy like you. We should talk
about your...what did you say? Gimmicks? Eisner? Iger?
Those guys have a whole staff to crank out pages. I have
the contacts, but to really make it, you have to be able
to produce.

FINGER
You want me to write for you?

KANE
Don't oversell it, I can write as well as anyone. I have to
make things happen, Bill. Right now. Hell, Will Eisner
has a stake in a whole studio, and I'm a year older than
him!

(KANE pours a little more for FINGER)

KANE
I draw, I have a portfolio. Concrete examples of my skill.
You're a writer, what do you have? A sheaf of papers,
a wall of words to dig through before an editor or
publisher can tell if there's any talent. What you need is
someone to take your ideas and jazz 'em up. You know
what they say, Bill. A picture is worth a thousand words.
I can do that for you.

(LOTTIE swans back in)

LOTTIE
Baahb! If you don't come dance with me, right now, I swear I will just die of boredom.

KANE
(Winks at FINGER) Well, we can't have that, my dear! Mister Finger, my new friend, will you do me the favor of holding my drink while I spin this fetching creature around the room?

(He hands FINGER his drink and takes LOTTIE in his arms)

KANE
I think we could help each other, Bill.

(FINGER watches them dance off)

(Lights shift)

Scene Three

(FINGER and PORTIA, who he has recently begun dating, are leaving a movie theatre)

(Projected: a poster for the 1931 DOCTOR JEKYLL AND MISTER HYDE)

PORTIA
Bill! It was terrifying! I can't believe you made me watch that.

FINGER
DENIER OF LIFE!! *(He playfully lunges for her throat)* MWAHAHAHAHAHAHAHA!

PORTIA
Oh, Bill…you are ridiculous. A monster movie…I'm sure just because you knew I'd jump into your lap.

FINGER
All of us have a dark side, Portia. "I learned to recognize the thorough and primitive duality of man; even if I could rightly be said to be either, it was only because I was radically both."

PORTIA

(Laughing) The things you say, Bill!...Did you just make that up?

FINGER

I wish! Robert Louis Stevenson, *The Strange Case of Doctor Jekyll and Mister Hyde.*

PORTIA

You and your silly monster stories...

FINGER

Before I met you, that was my whole life. Does that make you think less of me?

PORTIA

A little, but you're cute, so I'll overlook it. Well, all I know is that Fredric March is a handsome devil. It was awful to see them mess up his face like that.

FINGER

What did you say?

PORTIA

I mean, he's no Jimmy Stewart.

(She realizes that FINGER has stopped)

PORTIA

Bill! What's the matter?

FINGER

What? No! Nothing at all...I just...Talking about the movies, it struck me...they all kinda look like Dick Tracy villains, don't they?

PORTIA

Jimmy Stewart?

FINGER

No...although...

(He shudders as if the idea is horrific. She playful smacks his shoulder)

PORTIA
I like Jimmy Stewart!

FINGER
Clearly...I was just thinking of disfigurement as metaphor. Revealing or hiding the tormented soul within.

PORTIA
Just promise me we'll see something nice next week, like "The Ice Follies of 1939."

FINGER
Joan Crawford? I'll be jumping into your lap.

PORTIA
What's wrong with Joan Crawford?

FINGER
She reminds me of a cat my sister had.

(Projected: a poster for a revival of 1928 THE MAN WHO LAUGHS, with a prominent picture of Conrad Veidt with his ghastly grin)

PORTIA
Ugh. That's just horrible, I can barely look at it.

FINGER
"The Man Who Laughs!" It's terrific!

PORTIA
So you say. I say it's revolting.

FINGER
It's Victor Hugo! The king orders this boy's face carved into a permanent smile. He grows up as a freak show attraction.

PORTIA

Wow, Bill. How romantic. Lovely after-dinner entertainment.

(*FINGER has stopped, and pulled his notebook from his pocket and begins scribbling notes*)

PORTIA

I like going out with you, Bill. I know I tease about the monster movies. Every other guy from the neighborhood just wants to go drinking, or — God forbid — to a ball game!

(*PORTIA notices he's stopped again*)

PORTIA

I'm just not used to a young man growing so *disinterested* so quickly.

FINGER

Oh! No, no...I just...I have to write these things down before they slip away. I just met this artist, Bob. He's already published, and I really think he likes me...it could be a big deal.

PORTIA

Yeah, well...I'm right here. I like that you're "artsy," Bill, but you are going to have to focus on me occasionally...

FINGER

Isn't it just more interesting if the bad guy is scary *and* a little bit tragic?

PORTIA

If you want tragedy, I can leave you standing here and go home.

(*FINGER realizes his error*)

FINGER
I'm sorry. I get lost sometimes.

(She takes his arm)

PORTIA
You're lucky you're cute.

(A kiss on his cheek)

PORTIA
Why don't you take your best girl for a drink. You can tell me all about how you and this Bob are gonna be a big deal.

FINGER
Where do you want to go?

PORTIA
Fraunces Tavern, or the Old Town.

FINGER
You're the boss, you pick.

PORTIA
Let's flip a coin.

(FINGER stops short. PORTIA tugs on his arm)

PORTIA
Come on, Bill.

(Lights shift)

Scene Four

(ROBINSON is illuminated)

ROBINSON
Y'know, this business...Especially back then...It was all about being in the right place at the right time. After Superman? If you could hold a pencil and make a deadline? You might find yourself with a job. Quality, originality? That was a distant, distant second, and everything...Literally everything...was last minute.

(Lights shift. Jerry exits. VIN SULLIVAN breezes into the room, followed by an assistant, RANDY, and KANE, who is lugging a portfolio)

(Projected: The National Comics Logo)

KANE
I appreciate your time, Mister Sullivan.

SULLIVAN
Call me Vin. I edit garbage, I don't manage a bank.

KANE
Anything you say, boss.

SULLIVAN

(Sighs) Would it be easier to kiss my ass if I dropped trou?

RANDY

You have a meeting with Donenefeld in fifteen minutes.

SULLIVAN

Got it, Randy.

KANE

I have the pages you wanted! Fresh Rusty and His Pals!

SULLIVAN

Great, at least it's on time. *(He flips through the boards)* Ahh...there's that Bob Kane "style."

KANE

Thank you.

SULLIVAN

It ain't Rembrandt, Bob. Don't break your arm patting yourself on the back.

KANE

Well, I think kids like things straightforward. Simple.

SULLIVAN

Right. We like to assume the audience is stupid.

KANE

I was, um...hoping you might have something else for me?

RANDY

We still need six pages for Detective.

SULLIVAN

Really, Randy? You think I don't know that?

RANDY
I was just trying...

SULLIVAN
...To be a pain in the ass. Go get me a cup of coffee!

(RANDY begins to slink out)

RANDY
(To KANE) Do you want...

SULLIVAN
He doesn't need any coffee!

(RANDY runs out)

SULLIVAN
Well, you're here and have a pulse. I have a slot in Detective starting with number 27.

KANE
I think I've heard something about that.

SULLIVAN
Don't be cute, it doesn't suit you. I need it Monday.

KANE
Monday?

SULLIVAN
I didn't stutter.

KANE
That's three days.

SULLIVAN
If you can't make it happen, we just brought Nodell in from All-American, I'm sure he has something. Or, hey, the next guy who walks in the door.

KANE
No! I have a lot of ideas...Something like Peter Pup?

SULLIVAN

In Detective Comics? What are you, slow? I need a mystery man. Superman is selling like crazy, and Donenfeld wants more capes.

KANE

That's not my usual thing...

SULLIVAN

This is where the business is going. Get on board or hit the bricks.

KANE

Vin, I don't want to be in Siegel and Schuster's shadow.

SULLIVAN

We're gonna ride this fad for all it's worth. You want to sell comics at National? You're doing long-underwear characters.

KANE

Another Superman...

SULLIVAN

Whatever. Switch it up a bit. I'm sure you can think of a new gimmick.

KANE

I have a bunch.

(Beat)

KANE

A whole book full.

SULLIVAN

Hallelujah. Bring it in Monday.

(Beat)

KANE
I have heard Siegel and Schuster are doing well for themselves.

SULLIVAN
Oh, have you?

KANE
Well, I heard Jerry just got that apartment uptown, on the park, even...

SULLIVAN
I am gonna nip this in the bud, right now, okay Kane? Let me assure you that, no matter what you've heard, you're not going to get a deal like Siegel and Schuster.

KANE
I'm just asking, boss...

SULLIVAN
Never. And their deal is none of your business.

KANE
I think it's fair to know the going rate.

(*RANDY re-enters with SULLIVAN's coffee*)

SULLIVAN
Siegel and Schuster are NOT the "going rate."

KANE
Come on, Vin, I bet even this kid knows what they're making.

RANDY
(*Blurts*) Eight hundred a week!

(*SULLIVAN shoots him a death look*)

KANE
Oh ho!

SULLIVAN

(To RANDY) The first rule in this business is "keep your mouth shut."

(RANDY grabs KANE's pages)

RANDY

I'll run these over to production.

SULLIVAN

Oh, will you? That's fantastic...

(RANDY runs out)

SULLIVAN

My wife's nephew. Too useless to ink, even. Driving me nuts.

KANE

We all hear the rumors.

SULLIVAN

Well, rumors are rumors. My nephew shooting his mouth off is stupidity.

KANE

Eight hundred dollars a week...

SULLIVAN

Look, Kane...I'll tell you this, you bring me a good gimmick, something that can ride this long-under-wear fad? We'll get you a square deal, but don't think you're gonna walk out of here with a gold mine. This is disposable entertainment at ten cents a pop. In ten years nobody's gonna care about Superman, let alone whatever cash-in you walk in with on Monday. Those Cleveland kids got lucky, and they're grabbing all they can get. Action, Superman, and I hear the McClure syndicate is even putting them in newspapers.

KANE
Really?

SULLIVAN
A daily strip. Can you believe that? One year ago they dreamed it up, and they're going to be in the Herald-Tribune right next to Milton Caniff!

KANE
Just three days?

SULLIVAN
Don't look at it that way...It's a whole weekend.

KANE
Monday...

SULLIVAN
Christ, Bob. it's not Shakespeare. Everything's "borrowed," half of Superman's out of the bible. Gangsters, gunrunners, evil scientists, you just need a gimmick. A good, solid costume and you're more than halfway there. Plus, you've got a whole book full of gimmicks, right? You put a guy in a strongman's outfit, give him a cape, bright colors...I hear Bill Parker and Chuck Beck are cranking out a guy for Fawcett... Captain Thunder or some shit. A kid turns into Fred MacMurray. *(Chuckles)* That's never gonna work. It's all about the tights, Bob. Figure that out, and you're half-way there.

KANE
For eight hundred...

SULLIVAN
I know you Bob, you can sell the hell out of yourself, but don't think you're Babe Ruth. You can't just call the shot. Hit the home run. Don't count money you don't

have. Think about bringing me something publishable
on Monday.

KANE
I can do it.

SULLIVAN
Prove it...First thing Monday. Pages. In my hand.

(Lights shift)

SCENE FIVE

(DRAKE appears)

DRAKE
I know virtually nothing about Finger's family. Just rumors and little things he said. It certainly didn't sound like a fun place to grow up, by any means. Unemployment, alcohol, maybe even a wicked step-mother, but...It was just really clear he didn't want to talk about it. He might've told me about a sister, or maybe two sisters... But I know that whatever happened, it cut deep.

(Lights shift. DRAKE exits. The living room in the home of LOUIS FINGER and his wife, TESSIE FINGER, FINGER's parents)

(Projected: The Unemployed Citizen Newspaper)

(LOUIS sits, gazing into nothing, a glass of liquor clenched in his fist. TESSIE knits. FINGER sits, distant from the older couple, jotting notes in his gimmick book. GILDA FINGER, his younger sister, enters in a party dress)

GILDA
Well, here I am.

FINGER
Gilda, you look amazing. Heartbreaker.

GILDA
You really think so, Bill?

FINGER
I sure do.

GILDA
I'm glad you came.

FINGER
Wouldn't miss it.

TESSIE
Well, it seems presentable. Turn around.

(GILDA *turns, showing off the dress*)

GILDA
It's the nicest thing I've ever owned. The bee's knees!

LOUIS
It fits. Great. Not as out of practice as you thought.

TESSIE
At least you sobered up enough to do something right.

FINGER
(*Whispers to GILDA*) It's Much nicer than the one he made for Emily...Don't tell her I said that.

GILDA
It's our secret.

LOUIS
I made the finest suits in the city.

TESSIE

Be careful with that dress, Gilda. That's three weeks of milk you're wearing.

LOUIS

I made a suit for John D. Rockefeller.

TESSIE

We know, Louis. You've told us all a dozen times over.

GILDA

I wish they would stop.

FINGER

Don't listen to them, Gilda. Talk to me. Who's the lucky guy?

GILDA

Arnold Rosenblatt. He's in my class. I couldn't believe it when he asked me!

LOUIS

If you showed me even an ounce of respect I wouldn't have to!

TESSIE

Maybe if you weren't so damn useless!

(GILDA notices FINGER's notebook)

GILDA

Are you writing another story? What's this one about?

FINGER

Nothing, yet. I just saw a poster that I thought was scary.

GILDA

Poster of what?

FINGER

A man with a permanent smile!

(FINGER twists his face into a rictus grin)

GILDA
Don't do that! It's creepy!

FINGER
That's the whole point!

TESSIE
Gilda, what did I say? Go take that dress off before you ruin it!

GILDA
Do I have to? It's so pretty.

LOUIS
At least someone respects my work.

TESSIE
Do it now! One tear or stain on that dress, and that Rosenblatt boy will realize you're nothing but trash. Then where will we be?

GILDA
Yes ma'am.

(GILDA slinks into the back of the apartment)

FINGER
You don't need to be so cruel.

TESSIE
Don't you tell me how to raise that girl! I didn't ask for you brats, and I certainly don't need backtalk from the likes of you.

FINGER
She's a child.

LOUIS
Well, you would know all about that.

FINGER
Says the man who hasn't been sober in a year.

TESSIE
Oh, you'll get there. Inevitable.

LOUIS
Well, Tessie, it seems my useless son, who can barely afford to pay his own rent, is ashamed of ME.

TESSIE
He's not the only one.

LOUIS
Shut your mouth!

TESSIE
What are you going to do? Hit me again?

LOUIS
Will it shut you up?

(FINGER gathers his things and makes to leave)

FINGER
Emily was the smart one, getting the hell away from here.

TESSIE
Don't bring up that name. Ungrateful brat.

LOUIS
Oh, you gonna run away, boy? Back to your retarded friends in the library basement? What a waste. A smart boy, who could've been a doctor or a lawyer, spitting in his family's face.

FINGER
If it wasn't for Gilda...

LOUIS
Two wasted years of chasing after your crazy little stories.

TESSIE
Scribbling nonsense in that little book of yours.

LOUIS
Wasting time and money on those god-awful pulp magazines. When are you going to grow up, Milton?

FINGER
I told you, my name is Bill...

LOUIS
I was a man! Provided for you and the girls. I had a shop, clients and honest work. Those bastards took everything in '29. My useless son won't even try to find a decent profession for himself.

FINGER
I have a decent profession.

LOUIS
A hobby for degenerates.

TESSIE
Gilda told us about how you ride around on buses all night, watching people. Staring. I'm surprised you haven't been arrested. That's what they do to perverts!

LOUIS
Sooner or later he'll ogle the wrong girl. And when you do, Milton? You can rot in a jail cell for all I care.

TESSIE
It might teach you something.

FINGER
"From childhood's hour I have not been
As others were — I have not seen
As others saw — I could not bring
My passions from a common spring—"

LOUIS
What the hell is that nonsense from?

FINGER
Maybe I wrote it.

TESSIE
(Laughs) It's out of one of those lurid books.

FINGER
It's Edgar Allan Poe.

TESSIE
Of course! Another degenerate.

FINGER
He was a genius.

TESSIE
Died penniless and crazy. That's how a pervert dies.

LOUIS
I know you think you're better than me. At least I had something, even if I lost it.

FINGER
At least I...

LOUIS
You have nothing! You embarrass me, and I don't want to hear any more about your stupid stories in this house. Is that understood?

TESSIE
Useless, broke and alone, just like your precious Edgar Allan Poe.

(FINGER exits)

TESSIE
You're a coward, Milton! Just like your father.

(Lights shift)

Scene Six

(MOLDOFF appears)

MOLDOFF

Well, the thing you have to understand about Bob? His parents doted on him, the sun rose and set upon him. He could literally do no wrong. His mother was wonderful. She was a saint, and his father was a smart man. He'd invite me over for dinner, and they would act like it was a holiday, or something. A spread like you've never seen. Biscuits, gravy, and hot apple pie…a la mode, no less! But here's the thing. Bob always got the best, no ifs, ands or buts. His mother would bring out the steaks? And if yours was this thick? *(He holds up his fingers about a half inch apart)* Well, then Bob's? It'd be at least this thick. *(He doubles the distance between his fingers)*

MOLDOFF

But…you couldn't blame Bob. He was told he was God's gift, and he expected it. I mean, I wish somebody had told me that! I might've done better for myself.

(Lights shift. MOLDOFF exits. The stage is now the Kahn apartment. HERMAN, KANE's father, is sitting in his easy chair, reading the paper. AGUSTA, KANE's mother, is making dinner in the next room. Sister DORIS is sprawled out on the floor with some paper dolls)

(Projected: The American Way Billboard photo)

(KANE is hunched over a stack of art books in the corner of the room. He has several flipped open in hopes of sparking his imagination)

AGUSTA
Dinner's almost ready! Herman, will you set the table?

HERMAN
Robert, if you're staying for dinner, why don't you set the table for your mother?

AGUSTA
Of course he's staying, Herman. I made his favorite.

HERMAN
Did you know he was coming?

AGUSTA
Oh, hush!

KANE
In a minute, dad...I have to find something...

AGUSTA
Herman, you know Robert is working. He has a deadline.

HERMAN
All my years at the Daily News, Augusta?...I know something about publishing deadlines.

(He gets up and begins laying out plates. DORIS wanders over to her brother)

DORIS
What do you have to draw?

KANE
(Spooky voice) A masked avenger!

DORIS
Silly.

KANE
Yep, but they sell!

DORIS
Why don't you do another Ginger Snap for me? I like Ginger Snap.

KANE
They're not paying me to draw Ginger Snap right now, Doris.

DORIS
Then just draw me one!

KANE
I can't right now. I only have until Monday to figure this out.

DORIS
Boo.

KANE
I will next week, OK?

(He holds up an art book with Leonardo Da Vinci's bat-winged flying machine prominently displayed on the page)

(Projected: The Da Vinci Flying Machine)

KANE
What do you think of this?

DORIS
For what?

KANE
A superhero!

DORIS
Like Superman?

KANE
Exactly.

DORIS
It's just a dumb ol' drawing.

KANE
It's a start.

DORIS
It doesn't look like Superman.

KANE
That's the idea, Doris. It has to be like Superman, but different.

DORIS
It looks like a bat.

KANE
It does, doesn't it?

DORIS
Bats are creepy.

KANE
But they can also fly...like Superman...

(KANE begins to sketch)

HERMAN
Y'know, Robert, if you didn't procrastinate so much, you wouldn't have to rush all the time.

KANE
I only got the assignment today...Vin Sullivan over at National wants another Superman.

HERMAN

National. Bunch of gangsters, if you ask me. That Harry Donenfeld is neck deep with 'em.

KANE

Their money's good.

AGUSTA

Still pays the rent, Herman.

HERMAN

(Laughs) What rent does Robert pay? I know how much you slip to him when I'm not looking.

KANE

Do you have any idea how much Siegel and Schuster make?

HERMAN

Those two kids with Superman?

KANE

Exactly!

HERMAN

The things kids'll fall in love with...Robert, I want you to listen to me carefully...

KANE

Dad, I do not have time...

HERMAN

Robert Kahn! You WILL listen to you father!

(KANE puts down his sketchbook and turns to his father)

KANE

What?

HERMAN

I've worked in publishing for a long time. I've seen the money men wave checks in front little guys for years.

Those checks always seem like a number that will last forever...

KANE
Siegel and Schuster are making...

HERMAN
It doesn't matter. Does this publisher own Superman?

KANE
Well...I guess so...

HERMAN
Don't guess, *know*. Before you walk into that office on Monday, know what you are there for.

KANE
To sell my character.

HERMAN
That's short-sighted, Robert. Don't think about next week, or next year, think about ten years from now.

KANE
Dad, this is a fad...

HERMAN
What if it isn't?

KANE
I don't...

HERMAN
Whatever National is paying those two boys is only the tip of the iceberg.

AGUSTA
Herman...the table!

DORIS
Dad!

HERMAN

I am trying to help the boy!

(AGUSTA enters from the kitchen)

AGUSTA

Robert knows what he's doing, Herman. He's our super-star. Give him a few years and he'll be buying us a house in Long Island! I made your favorite, Robert...a nice juicy steak. Medium rare.

KANE

I have to work, mother. I can't stay.

AGUSTA

Well, then I'll wrap it up for you, and you can warm it up when you get home. Anything my handsome boy needs.

HERMAN

Agusta, you're going to smother the boy.

AGUSTA

So what if I do? Our Robert is special. He's going to be world famous. *(To KANE)* You just remember, son, anything in this world that comes to you? You deserve, because you are the best child any mother could ever want.

DORIS

How come you only make my favorite on my birthday?

AGUSTA

Don't sass, missy, or you won't get it then! Go set the table, since your father is being lazy. We need to give Robert room to work.

(AGUSTA and DORIS retreat into the other room)

HERMAN

Robert...listen to me. Remember, what you come up with? It's yours. Keep your name on it. Then they can't take it away from you.

(Lights shift)

Scene Seven

(FINGER's apartment. He sits in an easy chair, reading a copy of "The Shadow Magazine." He occasionally stops and jots down a note in his book. He stands and begins to pace, "performing" from the pulp magazine)

(Projected: The cover of THE SHADOW #113 - "Partners of Peril")

FINGER
"I've had his help on dozens of cases. I've never been able to find out his identity. He remains anonymous, by his own wishes. But whoever he is, I'd say he's the cleverest and most daring detective in America!" *(He drops the performance, and chuckles at himself)* I envy you Maxwell Grant, if that is your real name, you're almost as good as Gibson himself.

(FINGER pours himself a short glass of whiskey)

FINGER
(a la the radio show) "WHO KNOWS WHAT EVIL LURKS IN THE HEARTS OF MEN!?!? THE SHADOW

KNOWS!!! BWAHHAHAHAHAHA!!"

(He plops back down in his chair)

FINGER

Someday, Billy-boy. Someday you'll get your chance.

(There is a knock at the door. FINGER gets up and lets in KANE, who is carrying a portfolio)

KANE

Good, you're home.

FINGER

Yes, you're lucky. My social calendar is overflowing.

KANE

I need your help. Big-time project.

FINGER

Big time? Lemme guess, more Rusty and his Pals bits? I got some stuff in the book...

KANE

Bigger than Rusty! Biggest thing I've ever gotten my hooks into. Vin Sullivan over at National wants another Superman.

FINGER

The costume fad?

KANE

Fad, schmad. It's where the money is. This is for National. Superman put them on top, and they want to stay there. And...I've got the guy.

FINGER

You've got the guy?

KANE

You bet I do! You have a drink for your ol' buddy Bob?

(FINGER gets up and pours a glass for KANE)

KANE
Cheap stuff?

FINGER
Bob. You get what I can afford.

KANE
Well, don't you worry, Billy-boy. You stick with me, and you won't have to sell shoes anymore.

FINGER
That's what you said about Rusty and His Pals.

KANE
Old news.

FINGER
And about Peter Pup.

KANE
Funny animals are dead.

FINGER
And Ginger Snap.

KANE
Forget all that! I have GOLD here. This is a big night, Bill.

FINGER
OK, let's see your guy.

KANE
Hey, don't rush me! I'm telling you, this is so good, it needs a great set up...

FINGER
At your leisure, Mister Kane.

(KANE gets up and starts strutting about the room)

KANE
As soon as Sullivan said Superman, my brain started turning. What do the kids love about Superman?

(Beat)

KANE
Huh? Come on!

FINGER
Well, that's a pretty broad field, but, at a guess, I think the idea that this milquetoast guy secretly has all this power...

KANE
Sure, sure...

FINGER
It lets all these kids who feel helpless, bullied, think that, maybe they're a hero in waiting.

KANE
C'mon, Bill...

FINGER
OK! Why don't you just tell me what you want me to say?

KANE
He flies!

FINGER
Flying, OK...

(Beat. FINGER expects more)

FINGER
Is that your whole revelation?

KANE
Sure. What else is there?

FINGER
He's also bulletproof, super-strong...

KANE
Kids. Love. The flying.

FINGER
You know, he doesn't actually fly.

KANE
Are you trying to be a wise guy?

FINGER
He jumps.

KANE
What?

FINGER
"LEAP tall buildings in a single bound!"

KANE
It looks like he's flying.

(Beat. KANE is clearly set in stone)

FINGER
So, your guy flies?

KANE
Exactly.

FINGER
Is that the entirety of your concept?

KANE
What do you mean?

FINGER
Well, "he flies" is a pretty generic power set.

KANE
Of course there's more than that...

(Beat)

KANE
He flies around...and STOPS CRIME.

FINGER
You've really thought this out.

KANE
What do you have, big shot?

FINGER
If he had a magic ring that let him shoot power rays, or
if he was a former pro boxer...

KANE
What about it?

FINGER
It suggests more stories and situations. Why don't you
just show me what you have?

(KANE brandishes his portfolio)

KANE
All right! So, I told you, after I talked with Vin,
I immediately thought about this flying gimmick. You
ever seen Leonardo's designs for a flying machine?

FINGER
Of course.

KANE
"Remember that your bird should have no other model
than that of a bat..."

FINGER
Right.

KANE
A Bat-man!

FINGER
(Smiles) OK, I'm with you. See, *that*, is a gimmick we can work with.

KANE
So...I give you...

(KANE pulls a drawing from his portfolio. On it is a man in a bright red costume, without any chest emblem. Stiff, black scalloped wings spring from his back and tether to his wrists. The mask is a simple domino mask, and the character's blonde hair flies free as he angles through the air. It's about as far from the image of The Batman we have known for the past 80 years as one could imagine)

(Projected: The image of Kane's original design)

KANE
BAT-MAN!!

(FINGER stares at the drawing)

KANE
Well?

(FINGER leans back, considering)

KANE
What do you think?

FINGER
It's all wrong.

KANE
What do you mean? This is my Superman.

FINGER
The bright red suit, the blonde hair, the unwieldy cape-thing, or whatever that is...Bob, it's wrong.

KANE
You're just jealous...

FINGER
No, no...you ARE onto something, Bob. When you said "Bat-man." That was great. Maybe I've been reading "The Shadow" too much, but that set me off.

KANE
How so?

FINGER
You remember that film, "The Bat Whispers?"

KANE
Riiight...Chester Morris?

FINGER
That's the one. The killer wore a costume...a mask anyway. With a cape.

KANE
Yeah, yeah. It was creepy.

FINGER
Unsettling.

KANE
(Seeing it) Mysterioso...

FINGER
He could flare it out. Looked a little like wings.

KANE
Bat wings.

FINGER
Cooking with gas! What if we took it further?

KANE
Keep talking...

FINGER
A big, black cape. Scalloped, just like what you have, but

cloth. I see what you're going for here, but it'd be like carrying around a kite...

KANE
It's how he flies...

(Beat. Again with the flying)

FINGER
I get it, Bob...But it's ridiculous. It can be like actual wings when we want the visual, and just a cape otherwise. *(Looks at KANE's drawing again)* The red has to go.

KANE
But Superman...

FINGER
Bob. We could make a total Superman clone easy, and Sullivan would be happy as a clam. Thing is, it'd go two or three issues and disappear.

KANE
If it's good...

FINGER
Bob, let's be honest. Schuster can draw rings around you, and you know it.

KANE
...He's no Canniff, or even Eisner.

(FINGER looks at him, beat)

KANE
...But you're right.

FINGER
Boy...I may have to write this down in my diary. Red-letter day. We need our own, solid, gimmick.

KANE
But...

FINGER
The red suit has to go. Superman is Superman. We need a guy who is singular. The same realm, but totally different.

KANE
Set it apart.

FINGER
Right. Superman is big and bright, launching himself through the air. Bat-Man...no, no no!...THE Bat-Man...

KANE
Ohh...I like that!

FINGER
...That sounds like a creature of the night. Maybe a little bit scary.

(KANE has begun sketching)

KANE
Okay, I am with you.

FINGER
(Laughs) Like Dracula.

KANE
Kids love vampires.

FINGER
Sure they do. *(Holds the original drawing up to KANE)* Would a vampire be caught dead in a red suit? I say... gray. Gray and blue. Now, this mask...

KANE
What's wrong with the mask?

FINGER
We want some mystery, right?

KANE
Right.

FINGER
What's mysterious about a blonde guy in a domino mask? It's "Bat-Man" right?

KANE
When he's flying, the hair can be fluttering, y'know?

FINGER
OK, Bob. Let's table the flying.

KANE
Bats fly. He's Bat-Man.

FINGER
So make him look like a bat! A full cowl, ears...ohh, no eyes! Just white slits. Is he even human? Who knows? Human...That's the ticket. The kids, they want to relate to these guys. They want to feel like they *could* be this guy, right? What if our guy tells all those kids wrapping towels around their necks and running around playing Superman they don't need powers to be a hero?

KANE
How can a superhero have no powers?

FINGER
There are kids out there, they feel helpless, and they dream that maybe, just maybe, they'll find out they were rocketed here from another planet, with powers and abilities beyond mortal man...Well, what if our guy tells them, what if *we* tell them...that's not important.

KANE
How?

FINGER
A normal guy, trained and skilled, but not bulletproof or super-strong. A keen mind, quick fists, and a scary costume and gimmick. The Shadow can "cloud men's minds," whatever the hell that means, but...other than that? He dispenses justice at the end of his nickel-plated forty-fives.

KANE
The Shadow?! C'mon, Bill, the pulps are old news.

FINGER
Half of Superman is lifted from Doc Savage and John Carter, the other half is Moses.

KANE
Hmm?

FINGER
Come on, Bob...An orphaned child sent down the Nile to the Pharaoh's daughter? Raised by apes in deepest, darkest Africa, or by farmers in Kansas?

KANE
So we should say he's an orphan?

FINGER
We'll figure that out later...

KANE
How about this?

(KANE turns over his sketch pad, and we see a figure much closer to the Bat-Man that was ultimately published. FINGER takes the drawing and holds it up)

(Projected: Batman as originally published)

FINGER
(Smiles) Bob...I think we now have a reasonable Bat-Man.

KANE
That's great, because I told Vin we'd have one on Monday.

FINGER
Monday? Why is stuff always last minute with you?

KANE
Don't shoot the messenger! Probably didn't realize they were short on pages until they got to paste up.

FINGER
Whoo…How many pages?

KANE
Six.

FINGER
Well, that's a blessing.

(FINGER picks up the copy of THE SHADOW he was reading)

(Projected: The cover of "Partners of Peril")

FINGER
I guess we need to improvise. "Partners of Peril." Well, we need a new title.

KANE
I thought you said we needed our own thing?

FINGER
That was before you told me we had two days!

KANE
You're just gonna steal the story?

FINGER
Once we make this deadline, we can move on. I promise you we'll put our own spin on it.

KANE

Honestly, Bill...I don't care. The check's good either way. Finger begins to pace the room.

FINGER

All right, so...Partners of Peril...Partners in a chemical company...A chemical plant...a chemical syndicate. "The Case of the Chemical Syndicate!"

KANE

Ohhh...I like it. Sounds like a gangster film.

FINGER

So, we can tear it down, and figure out how to stick Bat-Man into it...We need a new way to introduce the character. Superman's entire backstory is laid out in six panels on the first page in Action number one. No mystery to it at all.

KANE

What do you have in mind?

FINGER

What if "The Case of the Chemical Syndicate" isn't the only mystery? A weird figure of the night...No one knows who he is..."A Mysterious figure..."

KANE

A mysterious AND adventurous figure.

FINGER

Heh...OK. "A mysterious and adventurous figure... fighting for..." I should write this down...

(FINGER grabs his notebook, and begins to scribble)

FINGER

"A mysterious and adventurous figure fighting for righteousness and apprehending the wrongdoer, in his lone battle against the evil forces of society..." *(He looks* at *KANE)* "HIS IDENTITY REMAINS UNKNOWN!"

(They laugh)

KANE
They wanted a mystery man.

FINGER
First panel; it's that text, and a shadow, a bat-winged shadow on a rooftop overlooking the city.

KANE
Yeah. That's great!

FINGER
Ok, we start with the Police Commissioner...It's Weston in the Shadow story...Weston. How about Gordon?

KANE
Does it matter?

FINGER
We can change it if I think of something better. Commissioner Gordon is having a drink and smoke with a friend...

KANE
A socialite friend, a rich playboy!

FINGER
A *bored* playboy.

KANE
I'm with you, like Don Diego in Zorro. Kinda foppish... no one would suspect his true identity.

FINGER
Cooking! With! Gas! We'll need a name...

KANE
Nothing ethnic.

FINGER
I'm not crazy. How about Bruce? Like Robert the Bruce?

KANE
Great.

FINGER
He's rich, monied...Old money... Should be colonial... Adams? Hancock?

KANE
Kane?

FINGER
Don't you think that's a little on the nose, Bob? How about Wayne?

KANE
Close enough.

FINGER
So, Commissioner...GORDON, and Bruce Wayne are having a drink, talking about this "mysterious Bat-Man." No one knows who he is, or where he comes from... The phone rings, and there's been a murder!

KANE
Wayne should be bored with it all.

FINGER
(*Laughs*) He's so bored, so utterly disinterested...He somehow invites himself into a crime scene.

KANE
"Nothing better to do!"

(*They both laugh*)

FINGER
The "chemical king" has been murdered, stabbed to death. His son's found the body.

KANE
His father should mutter something important to the
boy with his dying breath...

FINGER
What kind of mystery do you think this is, Bob?
Of course he does!

(FINGER is on his feet, and begins "acting out" the story)

FINGER
Someone's ransacked the room, cracked the safe, then
slipped out the window as the son came in...His father
mutters "Contract" to the son, and dies! The phone
rings! The guy's partner has also received a death threat!
The Commissioner heads there...

KANE
With great haste, even!

FINGER
Which seems like a pretty good time for Mister Wayne
to get bored enough to go home.

KANE
Or so it seems!

FINGER
Or! So! It! Seems! At the partner's house a gunman
appears! He shoots the partner dead, steals a document
and escapes out the window!

KANE
Bat-Man's there!

(KANE leaps up and strikes a dramatically heroic pose)

(Projected: A Batman Silhouette 1)

FINGER
"THE BAT-MAN!!"

(The two men rough-house a bit in mock battle)

KANE
Take that, evildoer!!

FINGER
No, no, no, Bob! A figure lurking in the shadows. A mysterious, SILENT figure!

(FINGER puts a finger to his lips)

FINGER
Bat-Man finds the stolen contract. Escaping into the moonlight just as the Commissioner arrives.

KANE
"Too slow, Gordon! Justice is swift!"

(FINGER rolls his eyes)

FINGER
We cut to the chemical plant. Two more partners hear the news reports of the killings.

KANE
This is complicated...

FINGER
Roll with it! It's a murder mystery, and it's only six pages!...There's a big henchman at the plant, he hits the third partner over the head and trusses him up in some sort of deadly contraption.

KANE
But the Bat–Man arrives!

(KANE leaps about. FINGER struggles as if tied up)

(Projected: Batman Silhouette 2)

KANE
Rescuing the man from certain DEATH!!

FINGER

The henchman, shocked to see this weird figure before him, reaches for his gun...

KANE

Bat-Man stops him with his quick fists!

(More rough-housing)

FINGER

The last partner arrives and reveals his guilt! Now he has to finish the job, pulling a knife...but Bat-Man grabs him.

KANE

The contract?

FINGER

An agreement to buy out the other three partners. Why buy what you could inherit!? The plot exposed, enraged, he desperately lashes out! With a mighty punch, Bat-Man sends him over a railing and into an acid tank!

(KANE, obviously enamored with playing the Bat-Man, again strikes a heroic manner)

(Projected: Batman Silhouette 3)

KANE

A FITTING END FOR HIS KIND!

FINGER

Our terrified victim turns to thank his shadowy benefactor...but he's GONE! Disappeared into the shadows of the night!! But the next day, we find Bruce Wayne, once again visiting the Commissioner for the "fairy tale" exploits of this masked vigilante.

KANE

But WHO is this strange figure really?

FINGER

"No one knows!" Gordon proclaims! But then at the Wayne home, the stunning reveal...Bruce Wayne IS The Bat Man!

(Both men look at each other. Beat)

KANE

That's good stuff, Bill. It's another Superman.

FINGER

No, it's not...It's Bat-Man. You think Sullivan will like it?

KANE

He's gonna eat it with a spoon.

(FINGER sits at his desk, setting a piece of paper to begin his script)

KANE

Bill.

FINGER

Yeah, Bob?

KANE

This is worlds better than what I had.

FINGER

Collaboration, Mister Kane!

(FINGER types away, KANE sketches on his pad, but stops and watches his friend work. The lights shift)

SCENE EIGHT

(*DRAKE appears*)

DRAKE
When we talk about Bob, I think a lot about Jerry Siegel and Joe Schuster. They were good guys. Fun to be around. Kinda naive, but good guys. I mean the famous story is that they sold Superman to Harry Donenfeld for a hundred and thirty bucks. Which is kinda true, and kinda not. Like a lot of things in this business. Jerry Siegel had a penthouse apartment on the park. He and Joe had contracts to churn out Superman that paid them better than anyone. They were rich! But Jerry still ended up broke and working in a mailroom by the time that movie with Chris Reeve came out in '78. Whatever you want to say about Bob? He didn't let that happen.

(*Lights shift. Drake exits. The office of HARRY DONENFELD, publisher of National Periodical Publications, KANE enters with SULLIVAN*)

(Projected: Image of cigars and deal-making)

SULLIVAN
Mister Donenfeld?

DONENFELD
What do you need, Vin?

SULLIVAN
This is Bob Kane, he's the one with the new Superman for Detective.

DONENFELD
Is he?

SULLIVAN
Yes, sir. It's not bad.

DONENFELD
So? Run it!

SULLIVAN
Well, there's a bit of sticking point...

DONENFELD
What?

KANE
I want a byline.

SULLIVAN
He wants credit.

DONENFELD
Nobody gets credit. We own what we publish.

KANE
I want the byline, and I want a cut.

DONENFELD
(Chuckles) The balls on this kid. I should throw you out of here. I got fifty guys who could bring me another Superman by five o'clock.

KANE
That's fine, I'm sure Dell or Crestwood would love my Bat-Man.

DONENFELD
Yeah? Will they after I drop a suit on you, *and* them, for stealing my concept?

KANE
How's it yours?

DONENFELD
Vin, did you ask Bobbie here to bring you "another Superman?"

SULLIVAN
Sure did, boss.

DONENFELD
Work for hire, Bobbie. It's mine already.

KANE
Hey, Vin...Did you pay me to whip up a story?

(No response)

KANE
I'm not your employee, Mister Donenfeld.

DONENFELD
You're a smartass, Kane. Hold on a second...

(DONENFELD sticks his head out the office door)

DONENFELD
JACK! GET IN HERE! You know Jack Liebowitz, Kane?

KANE
Can't say I've had the pleasure.

DONENFELD
Jack's my partner. He cooks the books around here.

(JACK LIEBOWITZ enters)

LIEBOWITZ
What do you need, Harry?

DONENFELD
Jack, this is Bobbie Kane...

KANE
Robert. Or Bob, please...

DONENFELD
Robert has whipped up a "new Superman" for Vin here, and he's got a few...demands.

LIEBOWITZ
Oh, does he?

DONENFELD
He says he wants credit...

LIEBOWITZ
We don't do that.

DONENFELD
And a piece of the pie.

LIEBOWITZ
We definitely don't do that.

KANE
I was thinking ten percent.

LIEBOWITZ
Are you fucking nuts?

DONENFELD
I defer to my partner.

LIEBOWITZ
If this thing, by some miracle, really is another Superman, we can talk about something, but...sight unseen? Not gonna happen.

KANE
Okay, okay. Ten percent? Too much. But I'm not selling out for a hundred and fifty bucks like Siegel and Schuster. You don't have to pay me the eight hundred…

DONENFELD
No way. Not if you put a gun to my head.

LIEBOWITZ
You think we're stupid, Kane?

SULLIVAN
Don't push it, Bob.

KANE
Fine, sure. I get it. How about this? Lets say this goes through the roof, five percent. If it doesn't work, you can pull the whole thing, and we go back to the drawing board… literally.

(LIEBOWITZ pulls DONENFELD aside)

LIEBOWITZ
Could be a good deal for us, Harry. Short term, anyway.

DONENFELD
Hell, the fad'll probably dry up next year.

LIEBOWITZ
Exactly. A piece of nothing is no loss for us.

(DONENFELD opens back up)

DONENFELD
Jack and I might be willing to entertain this…

KANE
In perpetuity.

LIEBOWITZ
Forever?

KANE
The name Robert Kane will be on every Bat-Man strip ever published. The fad dries up next month, but you bring him back in three years? Still my name on it.

DONENFELD
...and your five percent.

KANE
Well, of course.

LIEBOWITZ
TWO percent.

DONENFELD
I like that better.

KANE
Three.

DONENFELD
Jack?

LIEBOWITZ
Could work.

SULLIVAN
Who pays your team?

KANE
What team? This is all ME. Every word, every line.

(Beat)

KANE
Even if it wasn't, that's my problem to worry about.

SULLIVAN
I see how it is.

KANE
Bat-Man is a Bob Kane creation, period.

DONENFELD
Jack, draw up a contract with Kane here. You make sure we get all the…uhh…"Bat-Man" stories we need, Kane.

KANE
Sounds fair.

(KANE stands and extends his hand. DONENFELD stares at it)

DONENFELD
Get out of my office.

LIEBOWITZ
C'mon Kane, let's get the paper drawn up. I'm sure you'll want a lawyer to look it over.

KANE
Of course. I'm not stupid enough to trust a handshake.

LIEBOWITZ
Only a fool would be.

(KANE and LIEBOWITZ exit the office. Lights shift)

Scene Nine

(FINGER is sitting on a park bench, and jotting notes in his "gimmick book." KANE enters)

(Projected: The "Edgar Allan Poe" sign at Poe Park)

KANE
Is this where you hide out?

FINGER
I like it here. Tradition, I guess.

KANE
Tradition?

FINGER
(Pointing) That's where Edgar Allan Poe lived. That little cottage over there? He wrote "Eureka" in that house. *(Smiles to himself)* "Because nothing was, all things are."

KANE
What does that mean?

FINGER
Oh, it's this crazy poem he wrote, but...the blank page.

To pluck an idea out of imagination and make it real. Give it voice and vision.

KANE
"Real" may be a reach, but my imagination is going to be on the cover of Detective Comics twenty-seven, anyway.

FINGER
They bought it?

KANE
Of course they did! I told you Vin wanted it.

FINGER
You did it, Bob. You made it happen.

KANE
Let's get dressed and go down to Greenwich, catch some jazz, pick up some girls, and get good and drunk.

FINGER
This is fantastic! Do they want more?

KANE
Of course they want more! This is only the start.

(FINGER *pulls out his gimmick book*)

FINGER
I have been thinking of ideas for three or four more strips.

KANE
Take it easy, Bill, we can take a breath and enjoy the moment.

FINGER
I just...I know I can do better than ripping off a Shadow story whole-cloth. I don't want people to read it and just think I'm a thief.

KANE
It works, and what do a bunch of greasy ten-year-olds know about writing?

FINGER
You and I, Bob. Together, plucked our ideas out of the ether, and we have The Bat-Man!

KANE
Yeah, about that...I want you to be clear on something, Bill. This is my character. I created it.

FINGER
Well, yeah, you had the name, of course, and you certainly sold it...

KANE
The byline is mine. "The Bat-Man by Robert Kane." I'm building a reputation based on my name. I can get a bunch of guys working together, a studio, and we're all going to make out like bandits.

FINGER
Under your credit.

KANE
This is no different than what Caniff, or Iger, do. It's how all of those studios work. You helped me refine MY character. That's important. It's important to me, and I am going to take care of you...But you work for me.

FINGER
Bob, I...

KANE
Is that a problem?

(Beat)

FINGER

Hell no, Bob! This is what I've wanted for my entire life. People the world over know The Raven, or The Telltale Heart. Now, you come into my life, and I'm like Poe. Two guys from the Bronx breathed life into The Bat-Man and he exists.

(FINGER looks to the heavens and yells into the air)

FINGER
I AM A WRITER!!

KANE
Shake on it?

(They grasp hands. The lights fade)

END OF ACT ONE

ACT II

SCENE ONE

(Lights fade in. ROBINSON appears)

ROBINSON
They call it the Golden Age, the kids out there. The "Golden Age of Comics!" But for those of us who were there? It just felt like hard work and crappy pay. *(Beat)* That's not true. That's me being grumpy. I think that sometimes people, young people...and God knows I don't want to seem like some old fart yelling at the sky here, but still...don't really understand the joys of camaraderie. We did work that still means something, together. Bob's name was on it, he paid us what he saw fit, but we had so much more fun together than he ever did.

(Projected: 1940)

(ROBINSON walks into the scene. A cramped office space, FINGER, ROBINSON, MOLDOFF and DRAKE are huddle together over a drawing of a playing card joker image)

ROBINSON
I don't know, maybe it works, maybe it doesn't?

DRAKE
It's a playing card. So what?

(Projected: A Joker Playing Card)

ROBINSON
With that kind of STUNNING imagination, Donenfeld
should have you writing the entire line, Arnold.

DRAKE
What is he? A guy that throws razor-sharp cards, or
something?

ROBINSON
Maybe!

MOLDOFF
It's nice line work, Jerry.

ROBINSON
Thanks, Shelly. What do you think, Bill? Is there a story
in this?

FINGER
This reminds me of something...

DRAKE
A playing card?

MOLDOFF
Y'know, Drake, sometimes the smartass thing is tiresome.

DRAKE
I'll let you know when I feel that way, Shel.

(FINGER is flipping through one of his gimmick books)

FINGER
You remember that movie "The Man Who Laughs?"

ROBINSON
Conrad Veidt?

FINGER
Exactly!

ROBINSON
Creepy as hell, if I remember.

DRAKE
Victor Hugo?

FINGER
Exactly. Look...

(FINGER pulls a photo of Viedt in make-up from his book)

(Projected: An Image of Conrad Veidt from THE MAN WHO LAUGHS)

MOLDOFF
Yikes.

ROBINSON
You think this is something?

FINGER
If we take this...

(He holds up the Viedt picture)

FINGER
...and cross it with this...

(He holds up ROBINSON's card image)

(Projected: The Joker again)

FINGER
...What do we get?

DRAKE
A nightmare?

MOLDOFF
Clowns always creeped me out.

ROBINSON
The Joker! Like I said.

FINGER
It's a good name, Jerry.

ROBINSON
I think he should be really dark, a murderer.

FINGER
A stone killer! Holding the city for ransom, maybe radio messages announcing his victims. It's certainly a contrast.

DRAKE
A bat versus a clown? Yeah, I'd say so.

ROBINSON
The visual's great, honestly.

MOLDOFF
Says the guy who thought it up.

FINGER
It reminds me of this clown thing out at Coney, too. It's good, Jerry, We'll show this to Bob.

ROBINSON
Lord, why?

FINGER
He's the boss.

DRAKE
Riiight.

ROBINSON
He'll just rubber-stamp it, like always.

FINGER
It's still his show.

DRAKE
You guys spend too much time kowtowing to herr ascot.

MOLDOFF
Then why are you always in here trying to get work?

ROBINSON
The ascot is pretty ridiculous.

DRAKE
Cesar Romero better look out.

FINGER
Enough, guys. Bob'll be in and we can go over this for Batman number one. We need a new villain.

(PORTIA enters)

PORTIA
Quit loafing, boys.

MOLDOFF
Hey, Portia!

PORTIA
Shelly, how are you? How's Shirley?

MOLDOFF
Wonderful. Always asks about you.

PORTIA
Give her my love.

MOLDOFF
Will do. Boys, I gotta head back over to All-American and finish up some Hawkman pages.

(He starts to head out, but leans over to FINGER in passing)

MOLDOFF
Hey, tell Bob that, with the new book, I'd be happy to
do some work for you guys.

FINGER
Will do, Shelly.

DRAKE
I'll come with you, Shelly.

FINGER
You want me to put a word in for you too, Arnold?

DRAKE
If Master Kane of the snappy neckwear wants my services,
he knows where to find me.

ROBINSON
You boys up for some nosh at Katz's?

DRAKE
That is your best idea all day, Jerry.

ROBINSON
Jealousy becomes you, Drake.

DRAKE
Ohhh! I'm Jerry Robinson! I thought up a killer clown!
I'm so smart!

PORTIA
Bye, boys!

(The three men exit)

FINGER
They may kill each other before they finish lunch.

PORTIA
Well?

FINGER
What?

PORTIA
Did you talk to Bob?

FINGER
He hasn't been in.

PORTIA
What are you going to say to him?

FINGER
Jerry had a new villain idea.

PORTIA
That's great, but you know I'm not talking about that. We're getting married, Bill. You need to start thinking about the future.

FINGER
I do.

PORTIA
I know you love working here, spinning tales with Jerry and Bob, but you need to plan ahead. For yourself, but also for us. Bob's a reasonable guy.

FINGER
Sure he is.

PORTIA
Then ask him for more. Or, go out on your own. Max Gaines is publishing you with All American. You don't need Bob.

FINGER
I know, but...it's Batman. It's mine as much as his.

PORTIA
Bill, you have to drop that. This is your chance to make your own mark.

FINGER
Why rock the boat? This, here, with the guys…It's what I've always dreamed of. So, he gets the credit.

PORTIA
Why can't you move on? There's parts of you, wonderful parts of you, in everything you write. *(Beat)* I love you, and I cannot wait to be your wife. You are such a good man, and I want you to see that in yourself.

(KANE bustles into the room)

KANE
Hello, all! *(Looks about)* Where's Jerry?

FINGER
He went to get lunch.

KANE
Ah, Portia! How are you my dear?

PORTIA
Lovely, Bob. How are you?

KANE
Never better! Just had a great meeting with Donenfeld and Liebowitz, they can't wait to get the second book out.

FINGER
Jerry and I have something cooking.

KANE
Well, I hope your young lady isn't distracting you…

PORTIA
I was just on my way out. Remember what I said, Bill.

FINGER
Always.

(They kiss, and Portia exits)

KANE
Lovely girl. What do you have for me?

FINGER
New villain. Something Jerry brought in.

(He hands ROBINSON's drawing and the picture of Veidt to KANE)

FINGER
Scary clown thing. "Joker." A murderer with a permanent grin.

(KANE hands the materials back)

KANE
Sounds great.

FINGER
Bob, I was wondering if we could talk about…

KANE
Bill, I just stopped by for a minute because I told Harry I would make sure we were on track. I've got a meeting over at Timely; Martin Goodman and his nephew, Stanley …something.

(KANE begins to retreat)

KANE
Keep up the good work! Tell Jerry I'll be back with the checks on Friday!

(He exits. FINGER turns to his papers, a moment of reflection, opens the desk drawer and pulls a bottle of liquor out and takes a swig. and begins to write)

FINGER
"Once again a master criminal stalks the city streets — a

criminal weaving a web of death around him — Leaving stricken victims behind wearing a ghastly clown's grin. The sign of death from the JOKER!"

(He downs another snort. Lights shift)

Scene Two

(DRAKE enters)

(Projected: 1958)

DRAKE
Bob became obsessed with success. His ambition really couldn't be contained. It was a beast to be fed, y'know? You can't blame him, really. Who doesn't want to be rich and, relatively, famous? But, as soon as things were solid, the books were cooking on all burners? You could bet he'd decide he needed something more...

(DRAKE exits. KANE enters with SAM SINGER, an animation producer)

(Projected: The Hollywood sign)

SINGER
Bob, great to have you here. The creator of Batman and Trans-Artist Productions seems like a profitable combination.

KANE
Well, Mister Singer...

SINGER
Sam, please.

KANE
Sam, I can't let DC just assume they're going to get every million-dollar idea. Plus, between you and I, Sam, comics are starting to feel a little small for my work.

SINGER
I would think they would, after all that Wertham press.

KANE
Exactly! Who wants to be associated with a degenerate art form? I have big-time ideas, far beyond comics. So I wanted to bring them to a big-time Hollywood producer.

SINGER
(Laughs) "Big-time" is…uh…one way to put it. I'd rather say "profitable."

KANE
Wouldn't everyone, Sam?

SINGER
That's the way I look at it, but, hey, some people call themselves "artists."

KANE
I like to consider myself adaptable, in that regard.

SINGER
The philosophy of a successful man, Mister Kane. Here's the deal; we're looking for a new animated property. Syndicated airtime fillers. Five-minute shorts. Time-killers.

KANE
Maybe we can talk about something for a network slot?

SINGER
Wrong company for that, Kane. Hanna-Barbera's got a corner on the networks.

KANE
I saw in Variety that they sold some caveman show for prime-time. I was hoping to get on the coattails of that.

SINGER
(*Laughs*) Not in this shop. We do cartoons like my girlfriends, Kane. Quick and cheap. Now, you *could* take whatever you have over to Bill and Joe, but I gotta tell ya. They cleaned out Warners when Looney Tunes shut down. They're generating *plenty* of in-house material.

KANE
Oh, not like *this*, Sam.

SINGER
You could take your chances, but those guys? Not wasting time in funnybooks.

KANE
A stepping stone.

SINGER
I have a contract for twenty-six shorts, just to start. If it isn't a complete turd, I can probably make a few bucks with whatever you've got in that portfolio.

(*Beat*)

KANE
Well, Sam, then you are in luck, because I have just the thing you need.

SINGER
So it's not a turd?

(*KANE pulls a large board from his portfolio. A drawing*

of a costumed cat and mouse. They ride in a cat-themed car that looks suspiciously like the Batmobile, and emerge from a cave)

KANE
I give you...Courageous Cat and Minute Mouse! The furry foes of felony!

(Projected: The Courageous Cat image)

SINGER
Cartoon animals. I see a lot of those.

KANE
Animals, yes, but also superheroes! Our heroic duo, protectors of Empire City, reside in the Cat Cave, awaiting the call of the Cat Signal on their television.

SINGER
Cat-signal?

KANE
High-Tech! Kids will eat it up.

SINGER
Cats live in caves?

KANE
The cave opening has cat ears. It's the Cat Cave.

SINGER
I see.

KANE
Emerging in the Catmobile, they do battle with the miscreants of the underworld, and keep the citizenry safe!

SINGER
So, this is the whole thing?

KANE

I'm telling you, Sam...this is a CAT-miss idea!

(Long beat)

SINGER

It sounds little familiar, Bob....I mean, I don't read comic books, for God's sake, but that looks a hell of a lot like the Batmobile.

KANE

It's Courageous CAT. Nothing to do with Batman. That's a cat on the front of the car. A CAT. He's a cat, a cat who fights crime. It's totally different.

(Long beat)

SINGER

They're stupid kids, it's not like they're gonna ask questions. I think we can sell this to Tele Features.

KANE

The Bob Kane magic! I will consider your offer.

SINGER

Don't get greedy, Bob. We work cheap here, I want your Corporal Cat...

KANE

Courageous Cat.

SINGER

Whatever. I'm not bending over for you. You may be hot shit in the comics, but no one out here knows you from Adam. You got that?

KANE

All I ever insist on is a square deal, Sam.

SINGER

OK. Verbal agreement. We get the lawyers going, iron out

the details and get this thing rolling. *(SINGER extends his hand)* We're all going to do all right for ourselves here. Welcome to Hollywood, Kane.

(They shake, lights shift)

SCENE THREE

(ROBINSON enters)

ROBINSON
I have no idea what happened between Bill and Portia. I don't think anyone did. She left, and he felt darker, like a man adrift…But the fifties were tough on all of us.

(Lights shift, ROBINSON exits. In their small New York apartment, PORTIA is packing up her things as FINGER sits watching)

FINGER
I don't want you to go. I need you and Freddy here.

PORTIA
You need us? Did you say you need us?

FINGER
Life doesn't work without you.

PORTIA
Well, that's really interesting, Bill, because you can't seem to make it work *with* us either.

FINGER
I know that the work isn't always steady.

PORTIA
You're an artist. I accepted that long ago. I loved you, in a lot of ways because you are an artist. The problem is acting like a man.

FINGER
Portia...

PORTIA
No, Bill! No. I know it kills you. I know it does, and I know why. The problem is, I've stopped caring. I spent years in this apartment trying to prop you up, support you...

FINGER
I know I was never good enough for you.

PORTIA
Enough! Bill, you were cheated.

FINGER
Bob didn't...

PORTIA
I'm not talking about Bob. I am talking about YOU. I am talking about how you cheated yourself. "I'm not good enough for you." It's an excuse for never standing up for yourself. Scraping by on the scraps that that man deigned to throw your way. You could've changed that, but you chose not to.

FINGER
I took every job I was offered...

PORTIA
You also spent every moment you could away from us. How many checks did you hide from me, Bill?

FINGER

I don't know what you mean.

PORTIA

Oh yes, you do. If our marriage meant anything to you, please, stop lying. That money was for us, our family, you wasted it for booze and carousing.

FINGER

I wasn't…

PORTIA

You weren't working those nights you didn't come home.

FINGER

I had deadlines.

PORTIA

For a writer you're a rotten liar, Bill. When did you ever worry about deadlines? Mort Weisinger calls here every damn week looking for his scripts. It's not like I didn't know about the bottle in your desk, or that girl. I accepted it for as long as I could, because of our son. Always assuming you'd grow out of it, or get bored.

FINGER

Portia, I'm sorry. You were always my rock. It was just a stupid thing.

PORTIA

Oh, I know that too, Bill. We've been married long enough to know who you are. Exactly who you are. You're weak. A weak, childish man.

FINGER

I hate it when you say things like that.

PORTIA

I hate a lot of things! You could dream up anything, but you'd let it bounce around in your head forever. You needed Bob, or me, to force you to do anything.

FINGER
Eventually, I would've...

PORTIA
The fact is, without Bob? You'd still be sitting in a dingy Bronx apartment telling yourself you were going to be a great writer.

FINGER
I never said I was a great writer.

PORTIA
THAT'S exactly the damn point! You always acted like everyone was doing you a favor. They didn't give you work for charity, Bill. You could've written anything, a novel, radio, movies, plays! I know your parents made you feel useless. It took me a decade to realize they weren't wrong. You didn't believe in yourself, and then I didn't believe in you anymore either.

FINGER
Portia, please don't go. I can be better.

PORTIA
Maybe. But Freddie and I don't want to wait around for it.

(She exits. FINGER is alone. He slips a bottle out of his jacket. FRED FINGER, his 10-year-old son, peeks into the room)

FRED
Mom's mad.

(FINGER slips the bottle away, ashamed)

FINGER
Hey there, little man. Come over here and see your dad.

(The boy walks to him)

FRED
Don't be sad, Dad.

FINGER
I wish it was that easy, Freddy.

FRED
Mom shouldn't yell at you.

FINGER
I know it seems strange, but Mommy has every right to yell at me.

FRED
Why?

FINGER
It's grown up stuff, Fred.

FRED
I'm grown up.

FINGER
I know, but be a kid a little while longer, willya? For your dad?

FRED
OK.

FINGER
How did your project go? Did you show everyone the stuff I gave you?

FRED
Yeah.

FINGER
Did the teacher like it?

FRED
She said I was making it up.

FINGER
What do you mean?

FRED
She said that she'd read an interview with the guy who made Batman, and it wasn't you.

FINGER
Bob Kane?

FRED
I don't know.

FINGER
Give me a hug, willya?

(The boy hugs his father, and the lights shift)

SCENE FOUR

(MOLDOFF enters)

(Projected: 1965)

MOLDOFF

The conventions. Hooo boy. I don't think any of us were ready for that. I'm still not, really. They were for kids. Read 'em, wad 'em, shove 'em in their back pocket, trade it, line your parakeet cage with it. We weren't ignorant, we knew they were being read. But saving them? Keeping them in plastic or whatever? I have to tell you, and I really don't wanna upset anyone here... that seems nutty to me.

(MOLDOFF exits. JERRY BAILS stands at a podium, welcoming the fans to this first gathering. FINGER sits to his side)

(Projected: Comicdom's Cult of Collectors article)

BAILS

I'd like to take a few moments to introduce Bill Finger to you. Bill's been a Batman writer from the very first.

Bill, what would your advice be for the young writer who wants to break into the comics field today?

FINGER
I would say that one of the prerequisites to writing for comics and television is a sense of the visual. There are times when an artist has to hurry up a page to earn a dollar, or may be in a bad mood, had a fight or something, who knows? And you've gotta kind of goose them along a bit and explain, very clearly, the angles and action you want.

BAILS
What about fans? What's your feeling about the response of fans to your work, do you enjoy it, or find it a little irritating?

FINGER
What fans? Nobody knows who I am. In the pulps, your name is there. In the comics, we're the great anonymous horde, the writers. We're the unsung ...something.

(Lights shift)

SCENE FIVE

(FINGER rises and walks to SHELLY MOLDOFF in the hotel bar. A young boy of about 14, MICHAEL USLAN, approaches them)

USLAN
Excuse me, sir...could I have an autograph?

(He holds out a Batman comic book from the '40s)

MOLDOFF
You bet! Wow, that's an old one! How'd you get this?

USLAN
I've got a lot of old books. I've been collecting since I was a kid.

(JERRY BAILS sidles up to the bar)

MOLDOFF
Since you were a kid, huh? Now you're an old man?

USLAN
Yeah, I've got a copy of the very first Superman, and the second Batman, too!

MOLDOFF
Oh, really? Say, how would you like to meet the man who created Batman?

FINGER
Shelly...

USLAN
Bob Kane?

MOLDOFF
No, no. The guy who really created Batman. This guy right here, Bill Finger.

USLAN
Wow. Is that true?

FINGER
Why do you do this to me, Moldoff?

MOLDOFF
Because you got screwed....Don't repeat that kid...

USLAN
Oh, I won't. Pinky swear. I have a Batman comic, too. Did you write this one?

FINGER
Y'know what? I did.

USLAN
Will you sign it for me? It'd be an honor.

FINGER
Who do I make it out to?

USLAN
Mike. Thanks Mister Finger.

(FINGER signs the book. The boy's mother, LILLY, yells from off stage)

LILLY *(off-stage)*
MICHAEL! EDWARD! USLAN!!

(She rushes into the scene)

LILLY
What are you doing in a bar?

USLAN
I was just getting autographs from Mister Moldoff and Mister Finger.

LILLY
We are going home. This place is terrible. There is a man passed out in the lobby.

MOLDOFF
Oh, don't worry about him. He works here.

LILLY
Come on, Michael. *(Begins to drag the boy out of the bar)* I cannot believe you just wandered into a bar. We are going home, right now. When you told me you wanted to go to this, I had no idea it would be in a flophouse...

(They exit)

FINGER
Well, there goes another lifetime fan.

BAILS
I guess next year we should budget for a nicer hotel.

MOLDOFF
Are you kidding? That kid will do everything in his power to come back next year.

FINGER
Rule number one. Offend the mother. Ask Bill Gaines.

BAILS
(To FINGER) Is what Mister Moldoff said true?

FINGER
Aw, I wouldn't say...

MOLDOFF
Yes, it is. Every. Word.

BAILS
I know you don't know me very well, Mister Finger, but I write for...

MOLDOFF
Jerry here has one of those fanzines.

BAILS
Mister Moldoff has been very kind with his time.

MOLDOFF
Mister Moldoff? I'm gonna rap you upside of the head if you call me that one more time. It's Shelly.

BAILS
Ok, Mist...Shelly.

MOLDOFF
Now you got it. *(Drains his drink)* Gentlemen, I hate to drink and run, but my wife's supposed to be out front in five minutes. Jerry? All this? It's a hell of a thing. Bill, give me a call, willya?

(MOLDOFF exits. BAILS hovers, trying to come up with a way to break the ice)

FINGER
Have a seat. You want a drink?

BAILS
Only if you are.

FINGER

I'm trying to cut back. Had an episode back in '63. My ex-wife told me I deserved it.

BAILS

I'm sorry, Mister Finger.

FINGER

Don't make ME rap you upside the head. Bill is fine.

BAILS

So, like Mister Moldoff...SHELLY said, I have this fanzine...

FINGER

Right. You kids remind me of the old days, science fiction clubs in the basement of the public library, a bunch of us trading half-baked theories about H. G. Welles and Edgar Burroughs. Pimply-faced kids with nowhere better to be, and nothing more exciting to do.

BAILS

(Laughs) That's fairly accurate. So you were a fan?

FINGER

Of the pulps? Action? Adventure? Ate. It. Up. The covers featuring half-naked girls didn't hurt, either. *(Chuckles with memory)* Bunch of kids, really. Everybody full of dreams of carving out our own little stories.

BAILS

About what Shelly said...Batman...

FINGER

Ahh, I wrote a lot of those, but I *also* had a hand in Green Lantern with Martin Nodell and Wildcat with Irwin Hasen. Stuff that was *mine*.

(FINGER sees the excitement in BAILS' face)

FINGER
Not that you, or anybody else, cares about that. Batman is *Batman*.

BAILS
Well, Bill...can I just be blunt?

FINGER
Do I owe you money?

BAILS
Um...no?

FINGER
Then speak your peace. It's your nickel.

BAILS
I've gotten a bit obsessed with tracking down the credits on these old stories. It seems, talking to guys like Shelly, that Bob Kane had an awful lot of ghosts working for him.

FINGER
Might be the understatement of the decade. Maybe he didn't put pencil to paper all that often, but his checks never bounced. You can't say *that* about everyone in this business. The thing that really eats at me...Ah, hell, you don't want to listen to me complain... *(Waves at a bartender)* Hey, buddy! Can I get a Makers on the rocks?

BAILS
Actually, I do! Very much. I love the behind-the-scenes details. The stories behind the stories, as it were.

FINGER
Well, the truth of it is....Bob only "created" Batman if you think of coming up with a name as creation.

(A bartender pushes a highball glass in front of FINGER, and he takes a long sip)

FINGER
Bob talked a hell of a game, and he could sell bacon to
a Rabbi. But he really didn't draw much of anything,
especially after the first few stories. He damn sure didn't
write a word of it.

(Beat. Another sip)

FINGER
If it wasn't for ME, Bob's Batman would be some
ridiculous blonde bohunk *flying around stopping crime*
and spouting dunderheaded puns.

BAILS
But the byline...

FINGER
Oh, his name was on it! He made damn sure of that.
He had the contract. Shelly drew a bunch of it, Dick
Sprang and Jerry Robinson, too.

BAILS
That's incredible.

FINGER
He had the name, I have to give him that. But the look,
the concept, the feel? It was me. I got the papers around,
somewhere. I kept everything.

(Another sip)

FINGER
Story after story that Bob slapped his little box on.
"BOB KANE" with the big "O." I always figured he was
compensating for something.

BAILS
I don't understand, why would all of you...?

FINGER
He held the purse strings! Bob got himself a sweet deal

from Donenfeld, and has been riding it for decades. Rest of us in crappy one-room apartments, cranking out scripts to survive.

BAILS
I've heard that Kane is pulling back even more.

FINGER
I don't see how that's possible, unless he got a rubber stamp for his signature.

BAILS
Moving out to Hollywood permanently. I assume because of the TV show.

FINGER
TV show?

BAILS
The Batman TV show. Haven't you heard?

FINGER
No.

(FINGER drains his drink)

BAILS
Yeah, some producer named Dozier snatched up the rights. It's gonna be on next year.

(Beat)

FINGER
Figures.

BAILS
I didn't mean to upset you.

FINGER
I'm only angry at myself, Jerry. You want to know about Batman? I'll tell you whatever you want to know.

(Lights shift)

Scene Six

BAILS
"If the truth be known, or a Finger in every plot:"

(Projected: "A Finger in Every Plot" article)

BAILS
Somewhere today in Greenwich Village there is a small piece of notepaper; tucked away in a desk drawer along with other mementos. It is mute testimony of a famous episode in the unheralded career of the man who gave life to Comicdom's most memorable cast of characters. Bill Finger is the man who first put words in the mouth of the Guardian of Gotham. He worked from the very beginning with Bob Kane in shaping, and reshaping, Comicdom's first truly mortal costumed character. When fans clamor for a return to the days of old when Batman was a mystery man who battled the underworld

in action packed, human-interest yarns, they are clamoring...if the truth be known...for the return of the Batman as created by Bill Finger.

(The lights shift)

Scene Seven

(DRAKE enters)

DRAKE
I did consider Bob Kane a friend. I really did. We had a lot of history, a lot of good times. You always hope they'll get older, mature, and want to get their fingers back into the work. I mean, I knew about his almost pathological need to elevate himself. I knew he was given to, shall we say "forgetting" about collaborators, but it's been said before, he wasn't alone in that. I guess you don't see how deep the swamp is, until you're stuck in it.

(Lights shift. A fancy restaurant in New York City. DRAKE sits at a table. He's been impatiently waiting. KANE comes breezing in...)

(Projected: Image of Maxwell's Plum in New York)

KANE
Arnold! Have you been waiting long?

DRAKE
About a half hour.

KANE

Well, I just flew in from LA. Working on the show, you know. Boy, my arms are tired.

(KANE laughs. DRAKE half-heartedly responds)

DRAKE

Well, isn't that nice for you.

KANE

Adam West is just a true mensch. Nicest guy you will ever meet.

DRAKE

You don't say?

KANE

And the girls! The Hollywood girls are amazing, Arnold. You have to come out.

DRAKE

Some day, Bob, but, right now, I'm here, trying to make this deal for us.

KANE

I'm here now, Arnie-boy! Give me the concise version.

DRAKE

So, I ran the idea up the flagpole at King Features, and they thought with your name, they might be able to pick up a few dozen papers to start.

KANE

Couple dozen? That's hardly worth the time. It's from the creator of Batman, for God's sake! They give you a number?

DRAKE

I think they want to see it first.

KANE

You tell them that Bob Kane's name is gonna be like gold.

Especially when the show hits. Ya gotta handle these stiffs exactly like I did with the suits on Courageous Cat. They're gonna want some Batman magic to rub off on them.

DRAKE
Y'know, Bob, this whole thing might be easier if you actually came to a meeting.

KANE
Arnold, baby, you can't dirty the general down in the trenches. Like you said, they *want* my name. I've got a million-dollar deal going on over at Fox with Dozier. That's gotta come before some rinky-dink comic strip.

DRAKE
You're talking about how I make my living.

KANE
Who do you think we can get to draw it?

DRAKE
I thought you were! I was selling this as your big return to cartooning.

KANE
Oh, I'm not cartooning anymore.

DRAKE
I mean, come on, Bob. Don't you miss it? You were....

(*DRAKE very quickly considers how to put it*)

DRAKE
...Such a *great* artist.

KANE
It's beneath me.

DRAKE
Again, my profession.

KANE
It's easy enough to find a ghost. I'm spending more of my time on fine art.

(Beat)

DRAKE
You're kidding.

KANE
You should come over to my studio. I'll show you my oil portraits. I like clowns. Y'know, like Red Skelton? It's all the rage.

(Beat)

DRAKE
You're kidding.

KANE
We should be able to find someone who can copy my style.

DRAKE
Your…"style?"

KANE
Young kids all over who want a foot in the door. I've got this kid over in Greenwich doing my clowns for me. Drops off one or two a week for me to sign. Looks just like mine! They work cheap and leave a bigger slice for us.

(Beat)

DRAKE
You're kidding.

(A young woman, VERONICA, approaches the table. She is dressed in a low-cut dress)

VERONICA
Excuse me?

KANE
Why hello! How can I be of assistance to such a lovely creature?

VERONICA
The bartender just told me that your name is Bob Kane.

KANE
That is correct, my dear.

VERONICA
And you drew Batman?

KANE
I do have to slightly correct you, sweetie…I am the one and only *creator* of Batman. The caped crusader leapt to the page from this hand! You are such a lovely thing, would you like to sit down and have a drink with my friend and I?

VERONICA
Oh, I couldn't do that, sir.

(KANE eyes her figure)

KANE
Call me Bob. We have an extra chair.

VERONICA
My brother just loves comic books, and Batman especially, and he'd be so excited if I could get your autograph for him.

KANE
Aren't you just darling? What's your name?

VERONICA
Veronica, Mister Kane, but my brother's name is Archie.

KANE
Veronica? Do they call you Ronnie?

VERONICA
(Laughs) Sometimes.

KANE
Well, I certainly hope you will allow me to.

DRAKE
Bob, I think...

KANE
Take it easy, Arnold...Ronnie, do you think your brother
would like an original Bob Kane Batman drawing?

VERONICA
Oh, he'd love it.

*(KANE pulls out a piece of paper from his valise, and
begins a drawing. A very simple, well practiced, and very
rote headshot of Batman)*

KANE
Lean closer, Ronnie...so you can see how it's done.

*(VERONICA leans closer, which also happens to bring
her cleavage more into KANE's line of sight)*

KANE
That's it. Much better.

VERONICA
That's so neat. I wish my brother could see this.

*(DRAKE is less than amused by all of this. KANE finishes
up, and scrawls his iconic "Bob Kane" boxed signature. He
holds the drawing out to her)*

(Projected: Kane Batman Sketch)

KANE
Say, Ronnie...why don't you give me your phone

number? Maybe I can do another for him, one I can take a little more time on.

VERONICA
Well, I don't know.

KANE
You wouldn't want to disappoint you brother...

VERONICA
Well, OK...

(She begins to jot down her name and number)

KANE
Maybe we could have dinner and take in a show.

VERONICA
Maybe. I'm not sure.

KANE
They always have a table for me at The Rainbow Room.

VERONICA
No one can get in there.

KANE
I happen to be able to.

VERONICA
Well, maybe...it's not every day I get asked out by a famous artist.

KANE
World famous, even!

(VERONICA exits. KANE watches her walk away intently)

DRAKE
Dear lord, Bob. You're old enough to be her father.

KANE
How could I see a woman my own age, it would be like dating my mother!

DRAKE
If we could just talk about King Features...

KANE
I do want to be clear, before we go any further...It's my byline.

DRAKE
(Sighs) And...there it is.

KANE
My name's on it. It's mine. The creator of Batman! My name is selling it. Now, I'll make sure you get taken care of, Arnold.

DRAKE
Is that what you told Bill?

KANE
Bill?

DRAKE
You know damn well who I'm talking about! *(He gets up and gathers his things)* I'm not a kid who needs a foot in the door, Bob.

KANE
Well, forgive me for thinking we could both make a little scratch here!

DRAKE
Sure, as long as YOU make more! I'd just prefer my "partner" not be planning to screw me over from day one. Oh, and by the way, you might want to read this...

(He throws a copy of JERRY BAILS' article at him)

DRAKE
A kid named Jerry Bails wrote that.

KANE
Who?

DRAKE
He's a fan. Oh, I know you don't give a shit about anybody East of Anaheim, so I'll sum it up for you: People are figuring you out, Bob.

(DRAKE exits. KANE picks up the fanzine reads a bit, and the lights shift)

Scene Eight

(KANE stands to address the audience, reading from his "open letter" in response to ROBINSON's article)

(Projected: BATMANIA fanzine cover)

KANE
We can call this story, "Inside Bob Kane, or will the REAL creator of Batman sign in, please!" The myth: Bob Kane is not the sole creator of Batman.

(Projected: The Batman Logo, noting "by Bob Kane")

KANE
The truth: I, Bob Kane, am the sole creator of Batman. I created Batman in 1939, and it appeared, if my memory serves, as a six or eight page strip in Detective Comics, and I SIGNED it "Robert Kane."

(Projected: The Batman Logo disappears, and the Kane signature begins to multiply)

KANE
It seems to me that Bill Finger has given the impression

that he, and not myself, created the Batman. If Bill co-authored and conceived, either with me, or before me, then he most certainly would have a byline on the strip along with my name, just as Siegel and Schuster had as creators of Superman.

(KANE turns and regards the multiple signatures across the screen)

KANE
Where is Bill Finger's byline on the strip?... It is conspicuous in its absence, no?

(Lights shift)

Scene Nine

(STERANKO enters)

STERANKO
I know EXACTLY what you're thinkin', kids! When do we get to the good stuff? When does Steranko enter this tale? Well, my henchmen, it's right here! I knew there were all sorts of untold tales, under-the-table deals and backstabbing, creative masterminds lost in the tides of time. The kind of stories you only hear when some of us ol' ink-slingers get together for late-night gab sessions and shop talk. And I thought that was something people…four-color freaks like you and I…might like to hear about.

(STERANKO slips into an informal meeting with FINGER and JERRY ROBINSON. STERANKO's holding court with a cocktail in his hand)

STERANKO
You boys want a drink? I'm buying.

FINGER
I'm on the wagon.

ROBINSON
That's good to hear, Bill.

STERANKO
(Indicating his drink) You mind?

FINGER
Not at all.

ROBINSON
I'll stand in solidarity with my friend.

STERANKO
So, you see, I have this project. Very ambitious project. I want to do the history of comics, multiple volumes, covering every facet. You two were there with Kane at the beginning...

ROBINSON
Literally.

STERANKO
And I want to pick your brains, you with me?

FINGER
Who'd want to read that? Nobody gives a shit about what we did.

ROBINSON
Well, I think it's great, Jim. Someone needs to define our legacy.

STERANKO
This is what I am saying. Everyone's on this Pop Art bandwagon, that bastard Lichtenstein ripping off our work left and right. That God-awful WHAAAM! thing of his? It's Irv Novick's work. We all know that. Outright theft. Literally swiped our art!

ROBINSON
I've been saying this for YEARS!

STERANKO

That sort of nonsense cannot stand, gentlemen, and this is my way of showing the world that Pop Art...Well, it started with you guys.

ROBINSON

It's nice to hear someone else actually call it art.

STERANKO

Of course it is! It changes lives! Listen, men. I've been from one end of this country to another. Every sort of dive and crappy fairground you could imagine as a magician and escape artist. I lived hand-to-mouth for more years than I care to remember. Ate out of trash cans! Total squalor, but I always had your books to pick me up. They were always there when it was darkest. When I was wiping away the blood and icing my bruises. Hell, Bill...becoming an escape artist? It's because of you.

FINGER

How do you mean?

STERANKO

All those deathtraps you'd put Batman and Robin into! The daring escapes, the quick thinking and physical skill! I wanted to BE Batman. All because of what you wrote. My whole life, everything I am, it's because of you!

(FINGER gives him a look)

STERANKO

Well, hey, you caught me...Not JUST you. Hyperbole is my lifeblood. All the guys who toiled away on what half the world thought of as trash. Books that that bastard Kefauver and that ghoul Wertham tried to brand as some sort of pornography.

ROBINSON
Bastard.

STERANKO
So, Jim Steranko's History of Comics! I want to set the record straight for the sake of history. All I need from you, is a few stories.

FINGER
No one cares. No one.

STERANKO
Listen, Bill. I'm not on a crusade. I am saying that I will help you tell your story. The straight dope, you follow me? Right from the horse's mouth.

ROBINSON
Bill, you and I both know what happened. What you and I did. Why not tell the truth?

STERANKO
You boys are talking about Kane. I'll be honest with ya, it sure seems like he's sweeping something under the rug.

ROBINSON
I don't think you'll get an argument here.

FINGER
Bob has a...vested interest in the status quo.

STERANKO
I want the full dish, how you all worked together, how the stories were worked out, how the characters came to be.

ROBINSON
How Bob took all the credit? You talk about Lichtenstein? Anything Bob might've actually put pencil to paper on? He traced. Badly. Then guys like

me? Shelly Moldoff? We would come in and do the real work! The man was a hack, and rode us all to his fortune. No one more than this man.

FINGER
Look, Mister Steranko...

STERANKO
Baby, you can call me Jim all day long.

FINGER
Well, Jim, I can't go down this road again. The thing about Bob, and you can't take it away from him, he saw the possibilities. In a way that, say, Siegel and Schuster never did.

STERANKO
Hey, hey, hey. I'm not on a crusade. I got no power to set a warm piece of apple pie, preferably a la mode, on your plate. What I can do is let you talk about how Bob owns the deed to the whole damn apple orchard, you follow?

FINGER
Y'know what all that Jerry Bails stuff taught me? It doesn't matter.

ROBINSON
Bails was a kid, Bill. He did what he could.

FINGER
And Bob steamrolled him. He had the paper.

STERANKO
Yeah, we've all heard about this contract, but no one's ever seen it.

FINGER
Why should we? It's between Bob and National, er... DC. That money's gone.

ROBINSON
Bill, this is an opportunity to...

FINGER
To what? Have Bob point at his name on the books? Bob. Has. The. Contract. He's got years of books and strips that say "Batman by Bob Kane." That's history. It's written. He wrote it.

ROBINSON
Someday, Bill, it's going to hit you how long you've hidden all this away, and it's going to be too late. I can't watch that. Steranko, I'm happy to sit down with you and tell you what I remember, just call me. Bill. It was good to see you.

(ROBINSON exits)

STERANKO
Bill, I think you're wrong. I respect your decision, but, baby, life is a fight. Are you with me on this? I learned that a long time ago. Life doesn't do squat for those who roll over and let it have its way.

FINGER
I have bills to pay. All I want is to keep writing... Look, I can tell you about Jerry, Shelly, how we worked...but not about Bob. There's no point. (Gets up from the table) I'm heading out to LA with Charles Sinclair tomorrow. Someone over at DC suggested us to Bill Dozier for the Batman TV show. It's a paycheck. Maybe I'll make rent next month.

(He starts to leave)

STERANKO
Waitaminute, Bill!

(STERANKO crosses to him)

STERANKO
Can you really not make rent?

FINGER
You mean at this very moment? No.

(STERANKO fishes in his pocket, pulls out a bill)

STERANKO
I got a twenty, and I want you to have it.

FINGER
I can't...

STERANKO
Now, you just hold on a sec there, bucko. You wrote the stories that drove my childhood, and brought me the kind of joy that only a ten-year-old boy can know. I owe you the life I created through sheer force of will. A damn good life, Bill. You, and your work, inspired that. I want you to remember what's about to come out of my mouth, Mister Bill Finger. Any time you see me, and you could use twenty bucks?

(He puts the twenty in FINGER's hand and closes his fingers around it)

STERANKO
I am going to give you that twenty.

(The lights shift)

SCENE TEN

(FINGER and his writing partner CHARLES SINCLAIR, have arrived in Los Angeles and are working in an office on the FOX lot, crafting two episodes of the Batman TV show, "The Clock King's Crazy Crimes." FINGER is at the typewriter, Sinclair is staring out the window)

(Projected: The Hollywood sign — 1960s)

SINCLAIR
I tell you, Bill, I can get used to being out here.

FINGER
You can't complain about the weather, that's for sure.

SINCLAIR
Or the view... Is that Ann-Margret?

(FINGER gazes over his shoulder)

FINGER
Sure looks like it.

SINCLAIR
That is a beautiful woman.

FINGER
Maybe Dozier can introduce you?

SINCLAIR
Yeah! Cory would LOVE that.

(FINGER heads back to the typewriter)

FINGER
Yes, I'm sure Ann-Margret would take one look at you and drop Elvis like a hot rock.

SINCLAIR
Hey! You never know.

FINGER
Yeeeah, but maybe you do.

(They laugh. The door opens and WILLIAM DOZIER breezes in, followed by KANE)

DOZIER
Boys, I want you to meet the man whose work brought us all here. Bob Kane, the creator of Batman.

(SINCLAIR rises to meet KANE, FINGER rises, slower, and does not approach)

SINCLAIR
Mister Kane.

KANE
Always happy to meet with the gents making my brain-child fly.

FINGER
Still stuck on the flying thing, huh, Bob?

(Beat)

KANE
Bill?

DOZIER
You two know each other?

KANE
Bill and I go way back.

FINGER
To the beginning.

KANE
Almost.

FINGER
Or, hell, maybe before. Depends who you ask.

KANE
I had no idea you were...

FINGER
DC put in a word with Mister Dozier. Which I appreciated. I guess they're looking out for me.

KANE
I'm glad of that.

DOZIER
How's the script coming? Looking forward to the table read next week.

SINCLAIR
We'll have it ready, Mister Dozier. Just working out a few gags.

FINGER
Gimmicks, actually. I like to call 'em gimmicks. Right, Bob?

(FINGER waves his gimmick book at KANE)

KANE
Actually, I have to run. Appointments all day, you know.

DOZIER

No time to go down to the set? I know Adam and Burt would love to see you.

KANE

Not today, Dozier. I have to go.

(They begin to exit)

FINGER

Hey Bob...remember that night in my apartment?

(Beat. KANE and DOZIER exit)

SINCLAIR

What the hell was that? He ran out of here like a bat out of hell. I thought you knew each other.

FINGER

We were friends, I guess.

SINCLAIR

You guess?

FINGER

I met Bob Kane when I was a kid. Suddenly, here was this guy with big plans, and the will to make them happen. It was like magic, beyond my reach. He was bigger than life.

SINCLAIR

Because of the ascot?

FINGER

(Snorts) Different decade, same bullshit.

SINCLAIR

HE'S a fake, Bill. You can see it miles away.

FINGER

Where were you in '39?

(The men laugh. FINGER stops short)

FINGER
Bob likes to pretend he IS Batman. The rich playboy, the swashbuckling adventurer, the caped crusader. It was never about the work. He didn't revere Milton Caniff because of his two-fisted adventure tales, he just knew the damn things made the man rich!

(FINGER sits at his typewriter, touches it)

FINGER
I loved it, Charlie. Every day of it. Every minute! Everything we dreamt up, Gotham City, Batmobiles, Batcaves, loyal butlers, adventurous sidekicks. Catwomen and Clown Princes of crime.

(He looks at SINCLAIR)

FINGER
I took Bob's name and half-assed flying obsession...

SINCLAIR
What? He doesn't...

FINGER
It is a long story, Charlie. I took that name, and made it live. I wrote those comics, Charlie. I did. *(Flips over the title page of their script)* This silly little show is the only Batman story under my name.

(Beat)

SINCLAIR
I can't erase the last thirty years, Bill, but I can do this...

(He takes the title page of script and scratches out the writing credit, jotting in a revision)

SINCLAIR
"The Clock King's Crazy Crimes" by Bill Finger...

(Projected: The title page for THE CLOCK KING'S CRAZY CRIMES*)*

SINCLAIR
...and Charles Sinclair. I mean, I can't let you have *all* the credit.

FINGER
Yeah. What kind of an idiot would do that?

(They laugh together. Lights shift)

SCENE ELEVEN

(Lights shift)

(Projected: JANUARY 18th, 1974)

(FINGER's tiny apartment. The lights are low, a TV glows. We can hear the opening of "The Six Million Dollar Man," which fades as the scene begins. FINGER pulls a box from beneath the couch, it's full of pulp magazines and old comic books. He pulls several out, laughing to himself)

FINGER
Oh man! I haven't seen you guys in years!

(He pulls out a copy of THE SHADOW #113 — "Partners of Peril")

(Projected: THE SHADOW #113 Cover)

FINGER
"I've had his help on dozens of cases. I've never been able to find out his identity. He remains anonymous, by his own wishes. But whoever he is, I'd say he's the

cleverest and most daring detective in America!"

(FINGER laughs. He picks through the other books. STERANKO, DRAKE, MOLDOFF and ROBINSON step on the stage, they remain outside the scene, in shadow. They are only silhouettes)

(FINGER picks up "A Princess of Mars")

(Projected: The cover of A PRINCESS OF MARS)

(In this scene, the dialogue of the shadow chorus and FINGER's recitation of Poe's "Alone" should overlap a bit. The action of picking up a new book, and continuing the poem begins before the prior section is completed)

ROBINSON
"Springing to my feet I received my first Martian surprise, for the effort, which on Earth would have brought me standing upright, carried me into the Martian air to the height of about three yards. My muscles, perfectly attuned and accustomed to the force of gravity on Earth, played the mischief with me in attempting for the first time to cope with the lesser gravitation and lower air pressure on Mars."

FINGER
"From childhood's hour I have not been
As others were — I have not seen
As others saw — I could not bring
My passions from a common spring..."

(FINGER picks up "The Hound of the Baskervilles")

(Projected: The cover of THE HOUND OF THE BASKERVILLES)

STERANKO
"A long, low moan, indescribably sad, swept over the moor. It filled the whole air, and yet it was impossible

to say whence it came. From a dull murmur it swelled into a deep roar, and then sank back into a melancholy, throbbing murmur once again. The peasants say it is the Hound of the Baskervilles calling for its prey. I've heard it once or twice before, but never quite so loud."

FINGER
"From the same source I have not taken
My sorrow — I could not awaken
My heart to joy at the same tone
And all I lov'd — I lov'd alone..."

(FINGER picks up The August 1934 issue of WEIRD TALES, featuring "The Devil in Iron")

(Projected: The cover of August 1934 WEIRD TALES)

DRAKE
"The muscles of his heavy bronzed arms rippled as he pulled the oars with an almost feline ease of motion. A fierce vitality that was evident in each feature and motion set him apart from common men; yet his expression was neither savage nor somber, though the smoldering blue eyes hinted at ferocity easily wakened. This was Conan, who had wandered into the armed camps of the kozaks with no other possession than his wits and his sword."

FINGER
"Then — in my childhood — in the dawn
Of a most stormy life — was drawn
From ev'ry depth of good and ill
The mystery which binds me still..."

(FINGER pulls out a copy of ALL-STORY MAGAZINE October 1912, featuring "Tarzan of the Apes")

(Projected: The cover of TARZAN OF THE APES)

MOLDOFF
"Tarzan of the Apes watched them for a while from his lofty perch in the great tree. There was much in their demeanor which he could not understand, for of superstition he was ignorant, and of fear of any kind he had but a vague conception. The sun was high in the heavens. Tarzan had not broken fast this day, so he turned his back upon the village of Mbonga and melted away into the leafy fastness of the forest."

FINGER
"From the torrent, or the fountain —
From the red cliff of the mountain —
From the sun that 'round me roll'd
In it's autumn tint of gold..."

(FINGER retrieves a copy of BATMAN #47)

(Projected: The Cover of BATMAN #47)

STERANKO
"I swear I'll dedicate my life and inheritance to bringing your killer to justice...and fighting all criminals. I swear it!"

FINGER
"From the lightning in the sky
As it passed me flying by—"

ROBINSON
"Criminals are a superstitious, cowardly lot, so I must wear a disguise that will strike terror into their hearts! I must be a creature of the night, like a...."

MOLDOFF
"As if in answer, a winged creature flew in through the open window."

DRAKE
"A bat! It's like an omen! I shall become a bat!"

FINGER

"From the thunder and the storm —
And the cloud that took the form
(When the rest of Heaven was blue)
Of a demon in my view."

(FINGER smiles, and holds the comic to his chest. Lights shift and the four shadowy men exit. He lies upon the couch. Lights start to fade)

FINGER

"To be happy at any one point we must have suffered at the same. Never to suffer would have been never to have been blessed."

(Lights fade to black)

Scene Twelve

(KANE enters, moving quickly through the room. STERANKO enters, following him)

(Projected: The Golden State Comi-Con logo)

STERANKO
Kane?

KANE
I'm not signing autographs!

STERANKO
My name is Jim Steranko.

(KANE stops)

KANE
Oh, ho! So you're the Ster-rinky kid.

STERANKO
Steranko. I've been looking for you all morning, Bob. I wanted a word with you.

KANE
I see your pages. I can't believe Stan Lee let you get away

with that. All the hidden imagery and acid trip garbage, the kids don't want that stuff.

STERANKO
They don't?

KANE
Nah. They want simple and straightforward. Like my Batman. And it is MY Batman, Jimmy.

STERANKO
Don't call me Jimmy...

KANE
I read your book, Jimmy, your "history of comics." The Batman chapter is damn near slander, I'll leave it at that.

(KANE lightly cuffs STERANKO across his cheek)

KANE
See ya later, Jim, baby.

(STERANKO catches KANE's hand)

STERANKO
Not one guy in comics, in the brotherhood of artists, writers, publishers, not one guy has a good Bob Kane story. Even with your patent leather shoes and that ridiculous ascot, we know a dime-store con man when we see one.

(He slaps KANE, hard, and the bigger man staggers in shock)

STERANKO
You follow? Bob, baby.

(STERANKO begins to walk away. KANE starts to collect himself. STERANKO stops short and turns back)

STERANKO
Do you even know?

KANE
You hit me!

STERANKO
He's dead, Bob. Bill Finger was a brilliant, creative writer, who gave you everything. He died alone and penniless in a one-room apartment, two months behind on rent. Nothing but a tiny black and white TV to comfort him as he slipped away on a dirty second-hand couch. Seems there was no one to claim the body, and he's probably buried in Potter's field under an unmarked grave. You didn't kill him, but you put him there, Bobby baby.

(STERANKO walks away. The lights shift, tightening on KANE, who rises, disheveled. No one has ever struck him before, and he is terrified that anyone has seen his weakness. He looks about, in a near panic. Realizing he's gotten away with it, he composes himself. Smoothes his hair and clothing, and straightens his ascot. His light fades to black. Curtain)

END OF PLAY

About the Playwright

Mark Pracht was raised in the mountains near Colorado Springs, Colorado. He is Alumni of the University of Nebraska, Kearney, and was a company member of the Sheleterbelt Theatre in Omaha, Nebraska. During that time, he helped develop and produce seven world premiere productions, including his own full-length play, *NEON*.

He's worked as an actor, director and playwright in the Chicago theatre community since 2001, and received the 2019 Joseph Jefferson Award for Best Performance in a Principal Role for his portrayal of Harlan "Mountain" McClintock in Rod Serling's *Requiem for a Heavyweight* at The Artist Home theatre.

His work has been produced in Chicago by Brown Couch Theatre company, where he served as Artistic Director, and Strangeloop theatre.

CHECK OUT THE REST OF MARK PRACHT'S FOUR-COLOR TRILOGY

THE INNOCENCE OF SEDCITION

MARK PRACHT

A 1950s Congressional investigation into the supposed link between comic books and juvenile delinquency effects the careers of three persons: William Gaines, the originator of the horror genre of comic books; Matt Baker, a Black closeted gay artist of romance comics; and Janice Valleau, creator of a pioneering comics feature starring a woman detective.

THE HOUSE OF IDEAS

MARK PRACHT

Its the 1960s, and Marvel Comics is redefining pop culture. Behind the scenes, two visionaries, writer Stan Lee and artist Jack Kirby, built a shared universe that changed comics forever. But as Marvel's fortunes climb, so do tensions between its architects. Who truly deserves credit for The House of Ideas?

CAPTAIN BLOOD
DAVID RICE

Unjustly sentenced to slavery on a Caribbean island, the bold Dr. Peter Blood falls in love with the lady of the plantation, the lovely Arabella Bishop. When Blood escapes and takes up the life of a pirate, it appears that fate has separated them forever...or has it? Filled with sword fights and pirate battles, love and treachery, and even a song or two, Captain Blood is a pirate adventure perfect for the whole crew!

CHURCHILL
RONALD KEATON

March 1946. After leading Britain and her Allies to victory in the European Theatre, Winston Churchill has been shockingly defeated for re-election as Prime Minister. Living in forced retirement, Churchill receives an invitation from President Harry Truman to speak at Westminster College in Fulton, Missouri, where he will deliver his legendary, emphatic "Iron Curtain" speech.

THE COUNT OF MONTE CRISTO
CHRISTOPHER M. WALSH

Framed by a conspiracy and torn from the woman he loves, Edmond Dantes is wrongly imprisoned for fourteen years. Escaping captivity, he enters the upper reaches of Parisian society, insinuating himself into the lives of his three tormentors as, one by one, he seeks to use their own secrets to destroy them in the guise of his new identity: the Count of Monte Cristo. A dark tale of intrigue and vengeance by epic storyteller Alexandre Dumas.

THE DECADE DANCE
JOSEPH ZETTELMAIER

A one-night stand becomes a ten-year journey as Rog and Nina navigate a relationship against the backdrop of a turbulent decade. A touching two-hander, carefully balancing nostalgia, romance, and humor as two people live unexpected lives.

DEAD MAN'S SHOES
Joseph Zettelmaier

A dark and hilarious western, with a dash of buddy-comedy. Notorious outlaw Injun Bill Picote has escaped from prison, along with a hard-luck drunk named Froggy. The unlikely partners endure trials and bizarre misadventures as they set out to right a terrible wrong.

DR. SEWARD'S DRACULA
Joseph Zettelmaier

Dr. Seward has cut himself off from the rest of the world after losing his lover and friends to Dracula. The Irish author Bram Stoker wishes to tell his story. Soon, a series of murders occur, very similar to the ones Seward fought to stop. A re-imagining of Bram Stoker's *Dracula*.

EBENEZER: A Christmas Play
Joseph Zettelmaier

It's a cold Christmas Eve in London, and Ebenezer Scrooge sits in a hospital room. 15 years have passed since his miraculous transformation by the Ghosts of Christmas. They are about to return for a final judgment. Based on Charles Dickens' classic *A Christmas Carol*.

EVE OF IDES
David Blixt

The night before his assassination at the hands of conspirators, Julius Caesar attended a feast. With him were Brutus, Cassius, and Antony. During the meal, Caesar was asked what he thought was the best way to die. Caesar answered, 'What does it matter, so long as it's quick?' Based on history and the works of Shakespeare, Eve Of Ides reveals the unexplored relationship between the main players of the age — Caesar, Brutus, and Antony.

FRANKENSTEIN
ROBERT KAUZLARIC

When an unexpected death shatters her family, Victoria retreats into the darkest recesses of her psyche in search of a way forward. To find meaning in this impossible loss, she brings a terrible creation to life — one whose existence threatens all hopes for the future. Haunted and hunted at every turn, Victoria must endure a nightmare journey of the soul in a quest for survival. A brilliant reimagining of the 1818 thriller by Mary Wollstonecraft Shelley.

HAUNTED
JOSEPH ZETTELMAIER

"The best way to know a place is through its ghosts." Michigan playwright Joseph Zettelmaier set out to collect a wide variety of ghost stories for this anthology play of true otherworldly encounters by Michiganders from Milan to Marquette.

HAWK'S TAVERN
LORI ROPER & RICK SORDELET

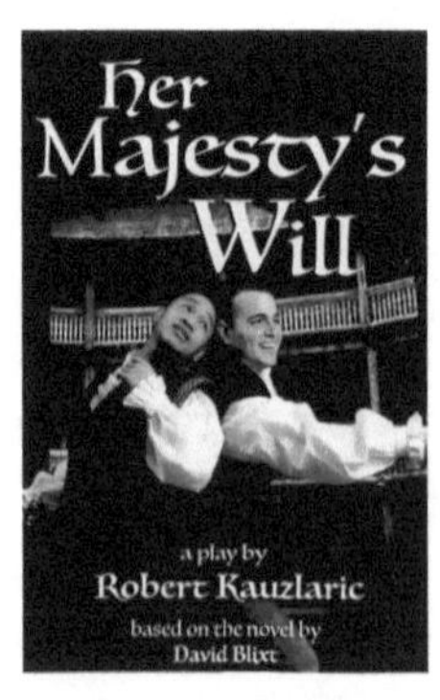

Hawks Tavern centers around estranged African American siblings who reunite amidst catastrophe. Together, they take on revolutionary measures while protecting the family bar amidst the tragic Newark riots of 1967. A bevy of family secrets set the stage for further turmoil in this comic-drama that which insists upon why we can't wait for social justice to heal the wounds suffered by the victimized.

HER MAJESTY'S WILL
ROBERT KAUZLARIC

Young William Shakespeare is hiding from the law in rural Lancashire, languishing as a simple school master. Christopher Marlowe is living the high life as a spy for the Crown. When a dastardly plot to assassinate the Queen draws these two unforgettable wits together, Will is swept up in a world of intrigue, treachery, and mayhem in an adventure that will define the rest of his life — if he can only manage to survive it.

IT CAME FROM MARS

Joseph Zettelmaier

A hilarious look at the night of Orson Welles' famous *War Of The Worlds* broadcast! The members of Farlowe's Mystery Theatre Hour are in rehearsal for their weekly radio show when they hear an alarming announcement come over the radio—Martians have landed! Suddenly secrets are revealed as the cast and crew believe it is their last night on earth!

THE LEAGUE OF AWESOME

Corrbette Pasko & Sara Sevigny

The superheroes of The League Of Awesome have done it again. They decided to punish the SorrowMaker by trapping him inside a Hardy Boys book. Yeah, it was a little unconventional. Zoe, Sylvia, Penny, Kitty & Rumble wouldn't let him escape. I mean....come on! They'd have to be drunk to do that! Now let's watch them celebrate their victory over him with mojitos. Oh...oh dear.

MALAPERT LOVE

Siah Berlatsky

A hilarious mash-up/homage/reimagining of classical comedic elements! *Malapert Love* is a modern response to the tropes, style and structure of Shakespeare's comedies. It follows the tangled and farcical action of a group of people who have all fallen in love with the wrong person.

THE MAN-BEAST

Joseph Zettelmaier

The wilds of France are stalked by a fearsome creature—the Beast of Gévaudan. An outcast forester presents its corpse to King Louis for a rich reward. However, the story he told may not have been the entire truth. Based on the legends of the loupe-garou, the famous French warewolf.

THE MAN WHO WAS THURSDAY
BILAL DARDAI

When Gabriel Syme joins the undercover detail tasked with infiltrating an anarchists' operations, he soon finds himself sitting on their Supreme Council with the code name "Thursday." It slowly becomes clear that no one in this battle between law and chaos is as they seem — and that Scotland Yard may have created the very problem they're trying to solve. Uncover the truth in this absorbing adaptation of the 1908 satire by G. K. Chesterton.

THE MOONSTONE
ROBERT KAUZLARIC

The Moonstone, an Indian diamond steeped in a history of violence and mysticism, is stolen from Rachel Verinder's sitting room, and no one in her household is above suspicion. Join an unforgettable collection of liars, lovers, addicts and outcasts as they struggle to uncover the truth and reclaim the stone before its curse destroys them all. This thrilling mystery by Wilkie Collins is regarded as the first detective novel in the English language.

ONCE A PONZI TIME
JOE FOUST

For years, Harold has 'helped' his friends with their investments, but his artful dodging and shady shenanigans are about to collapse around him as his pyramid scheme tumbles to earth. With only the help of his flakey father, his naive nephew, and a ventriloquist's dummy, can Harold hoodwink the Russian mob, bamboozle the SEC, and restore his friends' fortunes without his entire world becoming a complete farce? Watch him try!

THE SCULLERY MAID
JOSEPH ZETTELMAIER

Having declared an uneasy truce in England's ongoing war with France, King Edward III and his nobles celebrate in Nottingham Castle. Unbeknownst to the king, a murder plot is being hatched in the kitchen by the lowliest of his servants, who seeks revenge to right the wrongs of a lifetime. Religion, politics, and questions of loyalty, all at a knife's edge.

ANTON CHEKHOV'S THE SEAGULL
JANICE L. BLIXT & ALEXANDRA LaCOMBE

This new translation of Anton Chekhov's classic The Seagull restores what most English-language versions of the play omit: humor. Considered a world-class humorist and wit, Chekov intended this play to be a Comedy. Translated by Alexandra LaCombe and adapted by award-winning director Janice L. Blixt, this is The Seagull audiences have been waiting for.

SEASON ON THE LINE
SHAWN PFAUTSCH

A novice assistant stage manager joins the crew of Bad Settlement Theatre Company for their make-or-break season. An aging artistic director is hell-bent on mounting the elusive perfect staging of Moby Dick. The play swings from soliloquy to action-adventure story as the young man grows to love the theatrical live, even a those around him pay the ultimate price for their pursuit of theatre's own great white whale.

A TALE OF TWO CITIES
CHRISTOPHER M. WALSH

The Reign of Terror sweeps through Paris, and two Londoners are confronted with impossible choices. Will aristocratic Charles Darnay abandon his family to protect an innocent man? Can depressive barrister Sydney Carton make the ultimate sacrifice for unrequited love? An epic story of resurrection and redemption, based on the 1859 novel by Charles Dickens.

VOICES IN THE DARK
JOSEPH ZETTELMAIER

Turn out the lights and shiver with delight at this anthology collection of seven short horror radio plays by renowned horror writer Joseph Zettelmaier.

THE MASTER OF VERONA

Cangrande della Scala is everything a man should be. Daring. Charming. Ruthless. To the poet Dante, he is the ideal Renaissance prince—until Dante's son discovers a secret that could be Cangrande's undoing. Thrust into the betrayal surrounding Verona's prince, Pietro Alighieri must navigate a rivalry that severs a friendship, divides a city, and sparks a feud that will produce Shakespeare's famous star-crossed lovers, Romeo & Juliet.

VOICE OF THE FALCONER

Eight years after the tumultuous events of *The Master of Verona*, Pietro Alaghieri is living in exile in Ravenna, enduring the loss of his famous father while secretly raising Cesco, the bastard heir to Verona's prince, Cangrande della Scala. But young Cesco is determined not to be anyone's pawn. Willful and brilliant, he defies even the stars. Meanwhile, far behind the scenes, a mastermind pulls the strings, moving the players towards a bloody finale.

FORTUNE'S FOOL

While the brilliant, wily young Cesco is schooled in his new duties, Pietro travels to Avignon to fight his excommunication and plead for Cesco's legitimacy, unaware that an old foe has been waiting for this chance to seize control of Verona for himself. Separated from everyone he trusts, Cesco confronts his ambitious cousin, a mysterious murderer, and the Holy Roman Emperor himself. A harrowing series of adventures reveal a secret long hidden, one that threatens Cesco's only chance for true happiness.

THE PRINCE'S DOOM

Heartbroken, Cesco turns his troubled brilliance to darker purposes, embracing a riotous lifestyle in order to challenge the lord of Verona, the Church, and the stars themselves. Trying desperately to salvage what's left of Cesco's spirit, Pietro Alaghieri hopes the intrigues of the Veronese court will shake the young man out of his downward spiral. But when the first body falls, it becomes clear that this new game is deadly, one that will doom them all.

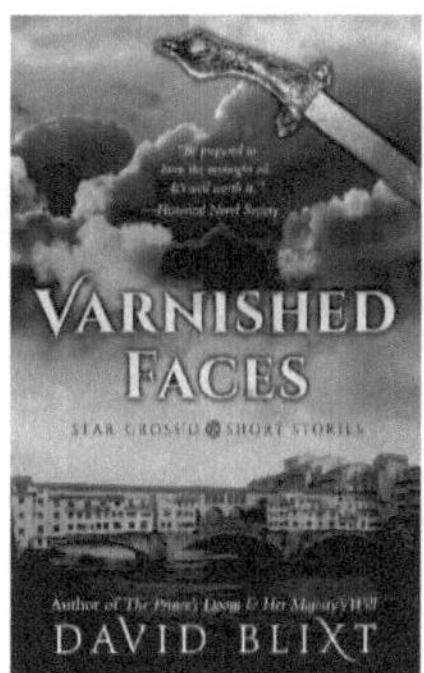

VARNISHED FACES

Collected here are several short stories from the acclaimed Star-Cross'd series, set both within Verona and the world outside its wall. Join Dante's son and Shakespeare's most mercurial creation as they live, love, and lose, seeking their hearts' ease. Filled with swashbuckling adventure, unrequited love, and brutal treachery, this epic journey recalls the best of Bernard Cornwell, Sharon Kay Penman, and Dorothy Dunnett.

HER MAJESTY'S WILL

England, 1586. Swept up in the skirts of a mysterious stranger, Will Shakespeare becomes entangled in a deadly and hilarious misadventure as he accidentally uncovers the Babington Plot: an attempt to murder Queen Elizabeth herself. Aided by the mercurial wit of Kit Marlowe, Will enters London for the first time, chased by rebels, spies, his own government, his past, and a bear. Through it all he demonstrates his loyalty and genius, proving himself to be - Her Majesty's Will.

COLOSSUS: STONE & STEEL

Judea, AD 66. A Roman legion suffers a catastrophic defeat at the hands of a band of Hebrews. Knowing Emperor Nero's revenge will be swift, they must decide how to defend their land against the Roman invasion. Caught in the turmoil is Judah: a mason who now finds himself rubbing shoulders with priests, revolutionaries, generals and nobles, drafted to help defend the land of Galilee. Denied the chance to marry, he turns all his energy into defending the besieged city of Jotapata.

COLOSSUS: THE FOUR EMPERORS

Under Emperor Nero's rule, Rome is a dangerous place. His cruel, artistic whims border on madness, and anyone who dares rise too high has their wings clipped with fatal results. For the Flavius family, this means either promotion or destruction. When Nero is impaled on his own artistry, the whole world is thrown into chaos, and the Flavii must navigate shifting allegiances and murderous alliances as they try to survive the year of the Four Emperors.

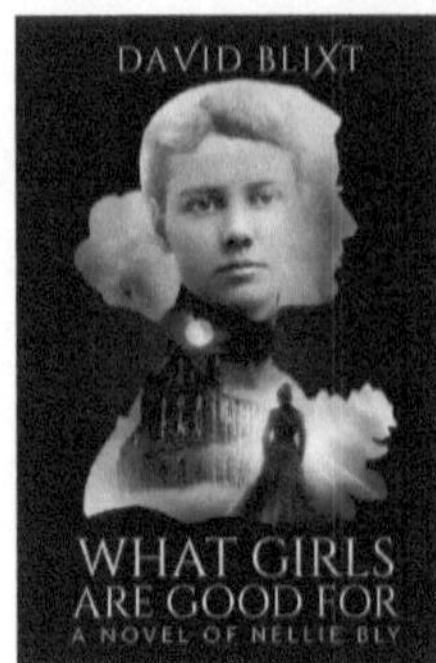

What Girls Are Good For
A Novel of Nellie Bly

Nellie Bly has the story of a lifetime. But will she survive to tell it?

Based on the real-life events of the tiny Pennsylvania spitfire who refused to let the world change her, and changed the world instead.

Charity Girl
A Nellie Bly Novelette

Fresh from her escape from Blackwell's Island, Nellie Bly investigates the doctors who buy and sell babies in Victorian New York. Based on real events and her own reporting, Nellie Bly asks the devastating question - what becomes of babies?

Clever Girl
A Nellie Bly Novella

A blizzard has frozen all of New York, and Nellie Bly is going stir-crazy when she and Colonel Cockerill plot out her most daring undercover assignment yet: she's going to trap the most crooked man in politics, Edward R. Phelps, the self-styled "King" of the Albany lobby.

Fighting Words

A volume of historical combat terms, as well as essays on broadswords, rapiers, smallswords, and storytelling. Including essays by David Blixt, Jared Kirby, and Mike Leoni, and a glossary of terms culled from The Fightmaster's Companion by Dale Girard.

OTHER WORKS FROM
SORDELET INK
WWW.SORDELETINK.COM

HOLD, PLEASE
STAGE MANAGING A PANDEMIC
RICHARD HESTER

A pandemic chronicle from the particular point of view of a career Broadway stage manager living in Manhattan. Part journal, part blog, these essays attempted to make sense of the crisis and what it was doing to us. By the end, everything had changed. What follows is a journey through one of the most fascinating periods in both our cultural and our personal histories.

NELLIE BLY'S WORLD
VOL. 1 - III

EDITED BY DAVID BLIXT

Bly's complete reporting, collected for the very first time! Starting with the stunt that made hers a household name, Nellie Bly spends her first year at the New York World going undercover to expose frauds, sharpsters and boodlers, interviewing Belva Lockwood and Hangman Joe, and traveling around the world!

DAISY THE LITTLEST ZOMBIE

AUSTIN TICHENOR AND GARY ANDREWS

Some zombies are big.
Some zombies are small.
But Daisy is the littlest zombie of all.

Join this hilarious and heartfelt tale by Austin Tichenor and Gary Andrews as Daisy the Littlest Zombie struggles to find the true monster within her.

www.ingramcontent.com/pod-product-compliance
Lightning Source LLC
Chambersburg PA
CBHW030858200726

48289CB00003B/810